BLUE LABEL

Turtle Point Press · Brooklyn, New York

BLUE LABEL

EDUARDO SÁNCHEZ RUGELES

translated by
PAUL FILEV

To Luis Tévez and Cristina Bárcenas

First Turtle Point Press edition, 2018

First published in Spanish in 2010 by
Libros de El Nacional as *Blue Label / Etiqueta Azul*

Requests for permission to make copies of any part of the work should be sent to:
Turtle Point Press
info@turtlepointpress.com

Library of Congress Cataloging-in-Publication Data is
available from the publisher upon request

Design by Ingrid Paulson

ISBN: 978-1-885983-57-2
eISBN: 978-1-885983-64-0

Printed in the United States of America

CONTENTS

BITS AND PIECES FROM
THE BACK PAGE
(ENGLISH, PSYCHOLOGY, EARTH
SCIENCES NOTEBOOKS, ETC.)

1

The plan at first sight seems simple: if I can prove that I'm a third-generation descendant of a French family, I might be able to save myself. I need to find someone I've never met. All I know is that his name is Laurent, and what's more, he's my grandfather.

2

Eugenia—my mom—thwarted my expectations of her usual dramatics. There were no attacks of hypoglycemia or laby-rinthitis. "I need to talk to Dad. Can you give me his phone number?" I asked bluntly. I thought she wouldn't speak to me for weeks after that. I imagined various scenarios: clonaz-epam, dizziness, asthma, or any of her other performances. She turned around and went into her bedroom. When she returned to the living room, she handed me a copy of the Sunday newspaper supplement. She'd jotted down the number in the margin. "Why do you want to talk to him?" she asked calmly, without hysterics. "I need to talk to him about something." I pretended to read the supplement. "If you're going to see Alfonso, make sure it's somewhere well lit, in public. Don't give him your phone number. Don't tell him where we live. You know that your father isn't well." Eugenia has always been a tactful woman, far too polite.

3

Jorge has the body of a child. He'll never be able to grow a beard or mustache. At best, every three days, six or seven evenly spaced hairs sprout on his chin. Little by little, I've stopped liking him. He bores me. He's corny and sentimental. I'd prefer it if he were frank and direct, more open and spontaneous, less considered. I'd like to be able to talk to Jorge, to tell him that I can't stand the same routine day after day, that I miss Daniel, that I hate my house, tell him about my father's disasters, or my crazy plan to find my grandfather, Laurent. We don't talk much in our relationship. Our feelings often get in the way.

I don't like smoking. Jorge smokes. He's proud of the fact that he started when he was twelve. His mouth tastes like an ashtray. A slimy film with a bitter taste coats his tongue. His saliva tastes like soy sauce. He says he wants to see me. I know he's lying. He just wants to paw me and undress me with the pent-up frustration of someone who's autistic. Jorge's intelligent. However, my body drives him crazy. His mind latches onto it, and he ends up behaving like an animal. I hate him. He doesn't talk, doesn't ask questions. He just leers at me. I really liked Jorge—once. He's the only boy I've ever kissed. I revealed my breasts to him without a trace of anxiety or shame. We were—we still are—awkward lovers. Sex, rather than being a pleasure, is just a distraction. The flesh experiences pleasure or pain regardless. The internet is the best school of anatomy. Natalia regularly sends me videos or photos of hunks. Jorge's quite plain. He's no great beauty. Eroticism on the web is airbrushed. Reality—with its textures, smells, and sounds—is a lot cruder. Besides which, daily life doesn't come with a soundtrack.

4

I don't like my house. In my literature textbook, I came across a poem by a man called García who expresses a similar hang-up: "I am not I, nor is my house now my house," or something like that. My mom worships and defends a family that doesn't exist. She talks too much. She thinks she knows me because we eat lunch together, and sometimes, dinner. Eugenia stopped living one day in April when Beto and Daniel—each in his own way—decided to leave home. She never says it, but I know that my mom utterly deplores my silence. She thinks I've been indifferent to our tragedy. I can't stand her public displays of grief or her policy of exhibiting her misery. Common courtesy between us has broken down. She asks obvious questions: "Did you do your homework, Eugenia?"— my mom and I have the same name —"Are you hungry, Eugenia? Do you want anything from the supermarket, Eugenia?" My communication with her is limited to the exchange of forced smiles, simple questions, and flat monosyllables.

5

"Alfonso. It's me, Eugenia. I want to talk to you. Call me. It's important." He responds with a text message: *Bar Juan Sebastian in El Rosal. Eight o'clock.* Around six, under a gray, stormy sky, I grab a cab. I once thought that Alfonso was someone important. In primary school, I had a certain pride in telling my classmates and my teachers that my father was an artist. Alfonso Blanc was some kind of actor or casting director in the nineties. When I was a kid, I went to the Venevisión TV studio with him several times. The heavens open up: a torrential downpour begins. As always, Avenida Libertador is inundated. The cabdriver stares at me with a sadistic expression and suggests shortcuts down dark alleys. Jorge sends me a corny message. The memory of Alfonso dredges up fuel smells. The stench makes me dizzy. I constantly curse the crassness of memory. Alfonso had a VHS tape on the living room table. My father liked to tell everyone that he was a professional singer. Whenever we had company, after the second drink, he'd turn on the TV and play that tape. It was totally embarrassing. Daniel would cover his ears and hide in his room. Alfonso would force his guests to watch his appearance on a talent show called *How Much Is the Show Worth?* At the end of his performance, some bald man—supposedly an expert—told him that the timbre of his voice was good but that he should work on his modulation. Also, an old woman with red hair complimented him on his "knockout" shirt and, after a sarcastic laugh, offered him a sum of money. It was awful. I know that my mom felt really bad. The guests didn't know how to respond. Feigning praise was impossible. Later, after the divorce, Alfonso would call me at home, faking

tenderness in a moronic voice: "Eugenia, it's your daddy."
(I've always loathed his use of diminutives.) "Listen, the day
after tomorrow I'm going to appear in a sketch on a program
called *Viviana at Midnight*. I'm calling to make sure that you
watch me. You know, your father's an artist." The worst
thing about those days was having to go to school. I was
convinced I was a real laughingstock.

"I want to escape from this shit. I can't stand the absur-
dities of these military goons. I've been checking out the
French Embassy website. If I can find Grandpa Laurent,
they might grant me French citizenship. I have to find him.
I want to talk to him. Tell me where he is." I can tell he feels
intimidated. My false nerve has worked. What a dive! The
place looks like a venue for bachelorette parties. A giant
banner announces the evening concert: "Boleros with Elba
Escobar." God! "How are you?" he stammers eventually. He's
thinner than ever before, as thin as a rake. Although he's a
young man, his complexion is sallow. He looks like a stray
dog, one of those three-legged ones that roam the streets.
He has lank, dirty hair and looks like a bum. What's more,
the stench of the Guaire River follows him around. His
forehead and his hands glisten with sweat. "You've grown,
Eugenia. You're a woman now." His double chin sags. It's
gross. I get the impression that, when he said the word
"woman," he was staring at my boobs. "How's your mother?"
he enquires sadly. "Do me a favor, Alfonso—just tell me
about Laurent. Where can I find him?" He lights a cigarette
and offers me one. I refuse. "I don't know where he is,
Eugenia. The last time I heard from him was after the incident with Daniel. He called to —" "I don't want to talk about
Daniel." Elba Escobar greets her fans and begins singing

a bolero called "Delirium." Alfonso takes his time before replying: "Laurent lived in a small town in Barinas or Mérida, I'm not sure which, somewhere over there. The place is called Altamira de Cáceres. I probably have an address or number at home. But I think you're wasting your time. You know that your grandfather's a strange man." The same old stories I've heard before. My grandfather's name, for some unknown reason, has always been shrouded in dark legends. "I think he lived in the house of a woman by the name of Herminia. I'll get the details and text them to you. Are you going to look for him?" "I might. I'm not sure." "How's school?" "Fine." "When do you graduate?" "Now, in July." "What will you do? What will you study?" "I'm not sure. I still don't know." "Can I do anything else for you?" "No, I don't think so." "Eugenia." "What!" Elba Escobar's wailing ends. She thanks the audience and makes a crude joke. The geriatric crowd applauds. "Nothing, dear. Nothing." Text message: Jorge (corny as always) says he misses me. Alfonso Blanc makes me want to puke. Around him, everything smells like gasoline.

6

One idea that produces a morbid curiosity in me is suicide. I like to fill my backpack with imaginary explosives and picture my body, laced with nitroglycerin, blown to bits in the school's corridors. If I had to choose the best place to kill myself, I think it would be Natalia's house: seventeenth floor, Santa Fe Sur. The balcony of her parents' bedroom overlooks the Eastern Freeway. The idea of free fall appeals to me. I wonder what there is to think about in mid-air, in the final flight before the fall, before some housewife—

who's speaking on her cell phone—lets out a bloodcurdling scream at witnessing a human form crash onto the roof of a car out front, splattering the windshield with formless extremities. Dr. Fragachán says it's normal at my age to have violent fantasies. I enjoy pulling his leg. Every week I exaggerate my phobias and manias. Sometimes I feel sorry for him. He gets all nervous. I think he likes me. Natalia reckons he does. After Daniel's death, everyone agreed that "loco" Eugenia needed therapy. It was meant to help me get things off my chest, talk, cry, scream, and if necessary, take drugs. When Dr. Fragachán told me I could talk about anything I wanted, I told him something that, even today, still makes me crack up. Natalia told everyone, and now, sadly, it's become a widely recounted anecdote: "My only problem, doctor, is that I masturbate every day. Other than that, it's all good."

School is a real drag. Mathematics, Literature, Biology, or History: it's all the same. During breaks, I escape to the end of the yard to make out with Jorge or to just watch Natalia smoke. The boring routine of school suggests that life is and always will be the same. The future is far off, the past and present are just snapshots of school dress code: white shirt for primary and middle school, blue for junior high, and beige for senior high. School is the only universe I know. My mother has always said that Caracas is a dangerous place, and for that reason, my urban geography is quite limited. I'm not familiar with downtown, nor am I interested in getting to know it. I've never been to Mount Ávila. Now, like most of my classmates, Jorge talks about preparatory courses and university entrance exams. I don't want to study anything. I don't want to do anything. Daniel used to say that, far away from Caracas, the world might be a different place. I'd like to believe him. If the whole world were like here, then God would have to be credited as being no more than a mediocre architect. Cristian, the history teacher, always browbeats us with patriotic speeches. He says you have to fight and stand up and be counted. He enjoys delivering terrible harangues. "Democracy" is his favorite word. My classmates generally watch him with thoughtful expressions—or so it seems—while he urges us to follow the examples of dead heroes. Cristian's final "lecture" was different. Not because of anything he said: he always repeated the same things. The difference was the reaction of the new boy, Luis Tévez: "Fight, my ass! What fight are you talking about? Hulk Hogan—now there's someone who fought." The snickers started after that. The teacher, however, wasn't laughing. "Yokozuna fought." Cristian stared at him dumbfounded. "Evander Holyfield fought. Why would anyone around here fight? Venezuelans have always been cowards. Roberto 'Hands of Stone' Durán fought too." The whole class was drowning in laughter at those comments. Cristian called for order, and then, just like in a bad movie, we were saved by the bell announcing recess.

7

Everybody's talking about the approaching Easter break. Natalia has invited us to her house in Chichiriviche. Then the cycle begins over again: pool, barbecue, sex, beer, spaced-out stoners, and nothing else. I don't feel like going to Chichiriviche. The truth is—I don't want to be with Jorge. Jorge says that that house is special, because it was there we made love for the first time. He never says the word "sex," and instead of "tits," he says "breasts." I don't know why he uses euphemisms to talk about sexual matters: for example, "a blow job" is "fellatio." When he's with his friends, he's foulmouthed and vulgar. In that environment, he calls things by their real name. But dating, bizarrely, imposes a certain amount of modesty on him. Natalia told me the same happens with Gonzalo sometimes. "The thing is they have 'sex' with whores, while with us—their girlfriends—they 'make love.'"

Luis Tévez arrived in January. He was a sort of dropout. From last year's graduating class—or something like that. I don't know why he had to go to Brussels. Apparently he did some type of course in Europe that would be recognized in Caracas and would allow him to get his high school diploma without any difficulty. The Ministry complicated matters, so he was forced to repeat the second half of the final year. Luis was much bigger than us—more adult, more grown-up. His beard looked real. In the beginning, he appeared to me to be somewhat pudgy and out of proportion. His small head contrasted with his broad shoulders. He was neither fat nor skinny, short but not a dwarf. (Jorge was much taller.) What he did have, in contrast to my "little friends," was the look of a man. His arrival gave rise to various myths about him. Rumor had it that Luis Tévez was well versed in alternative sexual practices and hardcore drugs. In reality, he was shy. He spoke to no one. He had a scar on his left shoulder, apparently the result of a bullet wound. Natalia fell in love with him at first sight. "Man, he's so nice, I adore him!" she'd say while trying to do yoga. Luis was indifferent toward us. The boys held conflicting attitudes: some admired him, while others hated him. Jorge belonged to the first group. Luis Tévez inadvertently became a role model. Everyone wanted to dress like him, listen to the same music that he listened to, use the same aftershave, smoke the same brand of cigarettes. Luis had the habit of wearing his shirt only half tucked in. This insignificant detail became, all of a sudden, the standard uniform. I never spoke to him. He never spoke to me. The day when he told the history teacher, Cristian, that a group of unknown boxers were the true fighters of history, he was different. I saw, perhaps, the most beautiful eyes—although I hate the word "beautiful"— that I've ever seen. They were a kind of sad chestnut, a melancholy russet, a homesick brown. (Colored pencils have these kinds of ridiculous names.) I never imagined that Luis Tévez would be the person who would help me find my grandfather, Laurent, or that I would go with him to the University of the Andes to interview a reactionary poet. Usual routine suggested that this Easter, like all previous ones, I would spend at Natalia's beach house, going through the same old rituals. My encounter with Luis Tévez would change everything. When, at the insistence of my mother and Natalia, I enrolled in the John Doe Preparatory Course—or some other gringo name such as that—I thought I'd signed up for countless days of boredom and a waste of time. That course was awful. However, it was there, by chance, that something different happened.

8

Once again we were conned: the preparatory course was a sham. The teacher, Susana, blinded us with false advertising. She coordinated a training course that was held on weekends. The classes would supposedly be delivered by a group of trained education specialists. Those "qualified experts" ended up being Susana's younger brother, a student of mathematics at the Institute of Industrial Technology, and a cousin from Barquisimeto, who was studying the second semester of literature at Libertador Experimental Pedagogical University. Eugenia, who fretted over my future, forced me to enroll. Natalia, Jorge, and the others did the course out of boredom. Every Saturday morning Susana handed us a stack of photocopies: exercises taken from the internet, lists of synonyms, difficult equations, etcetera. Susana's brother, whose name I've forgotten, was a real character. The class put him on edge. Natalia, in particular, unnerved him. She liked to wear short skirts and make him feel uncomfortable with suggestive movements. Those were the most useless mornings of my life. Luckily, I had my iPod. Luis Tévez enrolled at the end of January. An interesting shake-up in routine occurred then.

The building where the preparatory course was held was really run-down. It was an old house that had been converted to accommodate a few stores, a bakery, and in the evening, a sort of gay disco, or as Natalia said, a venue with "ambience." The John Doe Preparatory Course was taught in what appeared to be a storeroom at the end of a hallway. That hall stank of marijuana, vomit, and piss. The Friday drunks from the disco would invariably be leaving to go home as we entered to improve our communication and numeracy skills. Susana's brother often delayed the start of class, borrowing a mop to clean up the mess on the floor. Next to the disco on the second floor was a sex shop called Kamasutra. Natalia was keen to check it out, but the invisible

dence. She enjoyed being crude and vulgar. She had a great talent for uttering obscenities and making lewd remarks. But, after copping an eyeful of hardcore images being shown on a TV, and walking around a stand filled with lubricants and "intradiegetic" pleasure pearls, her open-mindedness failed her. Mel and Luis weren't even looking at us. Natalia wanted to get their attention. She grabbed a huge tub of banana-flavored gel—or something like that—and steered me toward the counter. "Hi. I want to take this." I'm certain that, for the first time, Luis Tévez took notice of me. Mel Camacho took the product, scanned it, and put it into a plain, dark bag. Then he gave me some unexpected advice: "Some customers have complained about this type of gel. Apparently, it can cause allergies. I recommend you use it with a condom. You can take these, if you want." Without giving it a thought, he placed a packet of Durex inside the bag. "Will you take them?" "Yes," I said, a little dazed. "You're in my class, aren't you?" Luis Tévez asked. I nodded. "You're Jorge Ferrer's girlfriend, right?" I said I was. I felt stupid. "This is my friend, Natalia." Natalia approached and introduced herself with the blank stare of a lobotomy patient. "Anything else?" Mel interrupted. "Some lube, a film? We've just got in some new stuff." "Anything with Belladonna in it?" I improvised, but with convincing assurance. He took out a box from a safe and placed it on the counter. Natalia continued standing there with an inexpressive face. Luis lit a cigarette and offered us one. I declined. Natalia accepted. "Did you know that Belladonna set up her own company called Evil Angel?" said Mel. "We've got some great stuff. I recommend *No Warning*. It's got the works: gang bangs, bukkake, lesbians, squirt."

lowed by questions. Tension. Then, when I don't supply a reason, he yells at me. I yell back at him. He tells me to go to hell. I tell him to go to hell. In his simple and one-dimensional universe, he tries to hurt me by making me jealous: he dances a stupid slow dance, a bachata, with a dumbass, private-school bimbo, who at one time—in kindergarten or in primary school—had been his girlfriend. It's true it hurt me. I always get hurt. Not by him. What hurts, I suppose, is my pride, someone making a play for my personal property. I'd be lying if I said I didn't want to grab her by the hair, drag her along the ground, and spit on her. The stuff of cultural upbringing and genes...I suppose.

Luis Tévez came at midnight. Three drunken clowns chanted earnest greetings to him. He parked his motorbike in front of the house and walked toward the entrance. The soundtrack of bachatas stopped him in his tracks, and he pulled a face. His state of "shock" made me laugh. I couldn't help it. He looked at me and said: "What crap." Every party I'd ever been to was the same: the same music, the same volume, the same stories, the same drunks. "Yeah," I said, for something to say, "it's awful." It was cold. Even though I don't like smoking, I accepted the cigarette he offered me. Luis took his black Zippo lighter from the pocket of his jacket and brought his hands to my face. We smoked in silence. He stared at me with a childish expression. I remembered our lunch, with him and Mel. That was a strange day. We didn't talk about anything. Mel Camacho spent the entire meal talking about porno films and giving blow-by-blow accounts of repulsive storylines. Luis had seemed to me to be trying to impress Natalia with entertaining anecdotes. Natalia is prettier than me; I know that, and it pisses me off. Natalia's

NIGHT

1

All nights are the same: the ceiling and Mount Ávila. My
mother had imposed a totalitarian regime dictating how late
we could stay out. Sanctions for breaking the rules involved
a series of chores. I know all about the curse of insomnia.
First comes the darkness, then the battle. During sleepless
nights as a kid, I had to listen to the fights between Eugenia
and Alfonso. I was a silent witness to freakish sideshows.
Frightened by the noise, Daniel would climb into my bed
and pull me close against his chest. I knew then that Eugenia
"mother" was a whore and that Alfonso Blanc was a moron:
in between half-formed sentences, they dished out the same
insults to one another repeatedly. Daniel cried. He was
always timid. His weakness forced me to put on a show of
strength, which everyone assumes I have, even though I
don't. Natalia says that nothing affects me. I've often thought
I don't know how to be happy or sad. It's true, I'm inexpressive. Jorge says that I'm a cold fish, that sometimes, when he
kisses me, it feels like he's kissing a dead person. Insomnia
makes it easy to brood over pointless things. Sometimes I

have a chat with Natalia or the odd acquaintance, but lately all human interaction bores me.

Even before he left home, Alfonso was scared of me. I learned how to freeze him with a look, to insult him the same way my mother did, to make fun of his pathetic wishes, his trivial aspirations. Not because I took Eugenia's side. She was of use to me: a vending machine dispensing food and cash. In the small hours of the night, during my childhood, after the cessation of hostilities—which, appallingly, ended with noisy sex—I concocted all kinds of tragic ends for the both of them. Alfonso I humiliated and did away with in all possible ways: I had him running down the highway in his underwear, wearing a Dipsy mask—the green Teletubby. Eugenia I bashed and violated with blunt objects. At the time, I wasn't quite sure what a "violation" actually was, but the brutality of the word served as a useful tool for my violent fantasies.

The nights during my adolescence were similar. Alfonso disappeared. His place was taken by Roberto—Beto. Our home life improved. Beto was a quiet, simple, easygoing guy. Nothing ever bothered him. He never raised his voice, and he never tried to buy us off with false praise. One April, Beto's patience finally ran out. I remember he stood by the front door, calm and unruffled, and said: "Eugenia, you're crazy. You and your kids would be better off in a madhouse." Then he shut the door and left. After that, the house went back to being a hellhole. Later, Daniel started "acting out," and Eugenia totally lost connection to the real world.

One night, during my latest bout of insomnia, I heard the name of my grandfather, Laurent, being whispered. Another night, a huge map of the world appeared before me.

Another all-nighter carried me into Daniel's bedroom, and, in the middle of all his things—his unmade bed, his Harry Potter books—I decided that I wanted to get the hell out of Venezuela. The small hours—a time of sad reflection, more than bitterness—were all alike: from the balcony—a view of Mount Ávila; from the mattress—the ceiling. One of the strangest nights of my life was the one in which I took off with Luis Tévez. It was different, exciting, unusual, full of strange characters and colorful scenes. When Luis parked the motorbike, I called Eugenia and told her not to worry, that I'd be staying at Natalia's place. It was 12:52 a.m.

We stopped at an arepa stand. "Tell you what we'll do: first, we'll swing by my place. I have to get my camera. After that, we'll go to Titina's house. I think they're having a reading today. And at 5:00 a.m., I have to be at Floyd's house to finalize an installation. Is that OK with you?" I nodded. Luis Tévez spoke through his nose, barely changing the tone of his voice, accompanying his words with brusque gestures. His hands—whenever there wasn't a cigarette stuck between his fingers—shook in a form of early Parkinson's disease. We shared a *cachapa* and a Coke. We talked about everything and said nothing. During our conversation, Luis's eyes appeared to be following the flight of an insect. My cell phone was filled with missed calls and messages: four from Jorge, three from Natalia. *Call me, bitch. Natalia.* I decided to turn off my phone.

2

All parents are the same. The lessons in life are plain and simple: perfect marriages, dysfunctional cohabitation, traumatic divorces, gender-based, interracial, and intergenerational violence. Beyond the formal differences, what these couples all have in common is the myth of the happy home: they all want to appear as one big happy family. Luis's family, although somewhat atypical, was no exception to this manufactured idea. We crossed the Eastern Freeway: Santa Fe, Santa Inés, Los Samanes, entered a mountain pass, and after that, I lost my bearings. We stopped at a tall building. Luis lived on the twenty-second floor.

When the doors of the lift opened, I saw an old man holding a stringed instrument. Luis's mom placed her index finger to her lips. Everyone at the party—about a dozen people—threw us dirty looks. Luis walked on tiptoes. A group of old people stared with bored devotion at the virtuoso mandolin player. A flan, some canapés, a vanilla custard slice, and a bowl of Doritos were on a table. The noise of our shoes on the parquet floor caused Luis's mom to reprimand us. The mandolin player was chewing the inside of his cheek and had the expression of someone experiencing a solo orgasm. In the middle of the room were some bottles of whisky, imported beers, a four-stringed cuatro, maracas, and a guitar. Two high notes announced the end of the piece. Applause, acclaim, cheers, exclamations. I don't know why, but I found the player disagreeable. He had a smooth, freckled bald spot that was sunburned. His horrible mustache covered his lips, and saliva foamed at the corners of his mouth. He put the mandolin down and requested a whisky. Then he hurled a few curses into the air and enthusiastically shouted a few rounds of "Hell, yeah!" Luis's mom referred to him as the "Maestro." Luis told me that the Maestro was a member of an important group. I'm not sure what it was called: Serenata Guayanesa, Ensemble

Gurrufío, El Terceto, El Cuarteto—something like that. They were fellow choir members of whichever group Luis's mom belonged to. They were celebrating someone's birthday that day. "Luis, greet the Maestro," the strange-looking woman said, rather anxiously. Multiple cosmetic procedures had ruined her face. Her skin looked like one big scar. Her hair had red tones. She shook my hand with indifference, not even glancing at me. She was awed by the Maestro. "What's up, Enrico!" Luis said with a barely disguised suggestiveness. The mandolin player called him "juvenile delinquent," while embracing him lewdly and cursing at him. The fans reached a consensus and requested another song. The Maestro allowed himself to be cajoled and, after a few lame jokes and obnoxious pleas, said that he'd play a piece by some Aldemaro Romero or other. Luis asked me to wait for him in the living room, apologizing for subjecting me to that circus of horrors. He said he'd grab his camera and that we'd head over to Titina's place straightaway. The Maestro played a pretty piece. Even so, because of his disgusting mustache and his bald spot, I just couldn't appreciate it. Besides, the faces of the other clowns who were listening reminded me of the expressions of the mental patients at the Altamira Sanatorium, where for three months, I'd had to do work experience.

Fortunately, Luis returned quickly. A huge camera dangled from his neck. "Ready," he said. "Let's go." Señora Aurora—his mom—told us we couldn't leave until the cake was cut. Luis made some feeble excuses. The group stood up and approached the big table. The lights were turned off. What a disgrace! I said to myself. I hate the "Happy Birthday" song. It's the stupidest song in the whole wide world. Some dwarf grabbed a cuatro and plucked a few chords. The birthday boy was a cross-eyed fatso, whom Luis suspected of being a hermaphrodite. Luis touched my shoulder, and we snuck out surreptitiously. They sang "Happy Birthday" in its Creole entirety: "Oh what a wonderful night,/It's the night of your birthday…" It was horrible. Before we left, I saw the Maestro place his hand on Señora Aurora's ass. I grabbed Luis around the waist, and the bike roared into life. Speed—I discovered that day—ignites a certain type of passion.

3

High schools abound in mythical figures: the history of every school is filled with stories of legendary characters. Like the famed student (the son of a deputy principal), who—along with three anonymous companions—once urinated in the cafeteria. Also famous is the legend surrounding Longo, the immortal Longo, who, supposedly aggrieved at having failed Graphic Design—a situation that couldn't be redressed—slashed the teacher's face with a utility knife. There are always rumors spreading around about nonexistent people, rebellious desires, wild antics, and heroes with absurd glories. It took me a while to figure out that we were going to Titina Barca's house. She was famous throughout all the schools in East Caracas. She was older than me, having repeated a few years. They threw her out of our school in eighth grade. After changing between various schools in the city—both public and private—Titina ended up studying in a popular dive known as the Open Classroom. The story that made her famous is a bit gross, so I'll just be direct: last year—or the one before that, I don't remember exactly when—the rumor got around that, during recess, they'd found some chick sucking the PE teacher's cock in one of the rooms at the Open Classroom. It was Titina Barca. It was also said that Titina wrote erotic poetry and that she'd won several literary competitions. Although I'd heard a lot about her, I'd never actually seen her. We went to a house in La Floresta. Luis asked them to open the garage, as he didn't want to leave his motorbike out on the street. The gate was opened by a guy with a familiar head of hair: Mel Camacho.

I couldn't believe it. Everything was totally different. Here were all the elite of the rumor mill. Besides Titina Barca, there was the black girl, Nairobi, and the guy with slick hair, Pelolindo Roque—Andreína Vargas's former boyfriend, who'd bashed some guy's head in from Class B. There were some unusual people, unique in their diverse assortment. A really cute girl, pale and slim, approached me and greeted me. She introduced me to a fat guy called José Miguel, and thanks to her, I was also able to shake hands with the black girl, Nairobi, a cult figure at all the school proms and the local cinema's matinee screenings. Luis said he'd go up to Titina's bedroom to dump his camera. Before he went, he suggested I be careful with Claire, my enthusiastic guide, as she was a lesbian and a radical feminist. I'd never met a lesbian before. That was something alien: a topic for discussion at school, but absent from real life. One time, I think, while playing Spin the Bottle, Natalia had to give Claudia Gutiérrez a peck, but that was just random. And once, on the internet, we saw a video of a couple of private-school girls kissing each other in a bathtub, but, beyond that, we knew nothing. We were quite naive.

Titina Barca lived up to her reputation: she's the most beautiful woman I've ever seen in my life. She greeted Luis with a kiss on the lips and told him that he'd arrived in time for the reading of *peomas*—dirty poems. Pelolindo Roque and Nairobi had read theirs already, but in fifteen minutes the fat boy José Miguel's presentation would begin. Claire gave me some rum and invited me to sit down beside her. Luis and Mel were arguing about something, but I couldn't make out what it was. Titina Barca began to dance alone to a song that really appealed to me: "Girl, You'll Be a Woman Soon." I made out as if I knew it, given that everyone said it was from the soundtrack to a famous film from the nineties. After Titina's performance—which everyone applauded wildly—Nairobi took the stage. She announced the reading of José Miguel's *peomas*. However, a sharp and repetitive ringing at the doorbell interrupted the bard before he could begin. "It's Vadier," they all said. "Vadier's arrived," Luis said to me in whispers. I knew then that the myth was true: Vadier Hernández existed.

One of my brother's school friends, Antonio Suárez—a real nerdy type, slim, sporty, had the highest grades, a math champion, etcetera—had told him about this weird guy called Vadier, who was in his class. Vadier had been thrown out of school in ninth or tenth grade. For their end-of-class celebration in final year, everyone got together at Antonio's place. It was one of those model homes. The señores Aurelio and Lidia Suárez were your typical idle parents, lacking in all vices, who organized lunches, meetings, and provided a moral compass for the ailing society of parents. Vadier showed up at that party at midnight. Antonio Suárez had a hunch that something wasn't right when Vadier asked him his parents' names. "Lidia and Aurelio," he said, without giving their titles. A bad feeling is generally a sign of inevitable misfortune. Apparently, Vadier approached the table at which the señores Suárez were seated, chatting with another group of parents, and—coinciding exactly with the end of a song—calmly and evenly said: "Señor Aurelio, Señora Lidia! Would either of you mind if I smoked a joint in your house?" Señora Lidia, who suffered from a heart complaint, fainted. I recalled this story when Vadier entered Titina's house. He barged in, heading straight toward the bathroom. Just as José Miguel began to deliver his *peoma*, Vadier called out: "Titi, can you tell me where the kitchen is, please?"

"Five Against One, or An Ode to Onanism" was the name of José Miguel's *peoma*. Dead silence. The group improvised a semicircle. Claire grabbed hold of my right hand but didn't apply any pressure to it. Her skin had a soft texture, and despite Luis's warning, her nearness didn't turn me off. I liked her. I didn't pay any attention to the first few verses. I was drunk on circumstances. I hadn't had much to drink. My intoxication resulted from the dissimilarity, from the contrasting behaviors, from the audiovisual clash between Natalia dancing reggaeton, Jorge playing dominoes, the usual idiots talking about soccer, and the irreverent group that I had joined that night. I panned happily over the faces of the strangers: Luis, Mel, Pelolindo Roque, Titina, plus the black girl, Nairobi. Incredible. Profound verses struck the impassive listeners. At the high point of the reading, I managed to pay attention: "Five against one, I fantasize/And my pubes are your pubes/And my balls are your breasts/And a small sheet of toilet paper / Is your mouth where I come." José Miguel began to cry. Nairobi stood up and called for an enthusiastic ovation. But the applause and cheers were interrupted by a foul smell. I covered my nose. "Christ, it's Vadier!" someone said. Titina ran to the kitchen. Prompted by Claire, I got up and followed the direction of the crowd. On reaching a long countertop, I could see Luis and Mel rolling around on the floor in fits of laughter. The overhead kitchen cupboards were all open. On the table were arranged various condiments and spices: marinade, curry powder, oregano, cinnamon, bay leaves, pepper, a stock cube, and some cumin. Vadier Hernández had been preparing a type of cooked joint. By the time we went back to the living room, the rumor that would later become legend had already been brewed: Vadier had smoked a curry joint. Life is weird: I never imagined that this freak would end up becoming one of my best friends. In that moment, he seemed to me like a retard, a buffoon, a cartoonlike character—from one of those second-rate Ecuadorian imitations of manga. "We'll leave at 4:00 a.m.," Luis said to me. "I've got to be at Floyd's place by 5:00 a.m. at the latest."

I'd never heard of Floyd. Luis told Mel that he planned to do the installation that morning. "Does Floyd have the stuff?" "Yeah, he managed to get twenty pounds," replied Luis. "What'll you do at Easter?" asked Mel. "I'm not sure yet." "Nairobi's cousin's got a place in San Carlos. They want to organize a 'happening.'" I decided to wander around the living room and listen in on various conversations. Claire told me I had the most beautiful nose she'd ever seen and said that she'd like to kiss it. "What—my nose?" "Yes, your nose." The expression on my face scared her off. My reaction was more one of surprise than disgust. Pelolindo Roque was telling José Miguel and some of the newcomers about how he'd scratched the car of an old actor by the name of Carrillo. "Carrillo—who's that?" I asked in a low voice. Pelolindo replied without glancing at me: "A two-bit actor from the eighties, who wanders around in a state of confusion with his army buddies. Samuel thought it'd be a good idea to screw him over." They toasted one another and laughed. Samuel—I wondered in silence—who could that be? Someone blew in my ear. It tickled. It was Luis: "How are you?" "Good," I replied. "Do you like the party?" "Yeah, it's good. It's much better than Gonzo's." "I'm sorry for taking you to my place. I forgot it was the birthday of one of my mother's boyfriends." "Don't worry about it. That party was better than Gonzo's as well." "You're not like them." "Like who?" I got nervous. I didn't know what to do with my hands. I picked up a plastic cup filled with rum and pretended to stir the ice in it with my fingers. "Our classmates," he said. "They're just a bunch of kids. I'm not saying that we're not pains in the ass. My theory is that we're all assholes, only they're bigger assholes." "Bigger assholes?" I felt like a fool responding with a question, but his way of speaking left me with no option. "Yeah, it's the truth, although there's one small difference: we're assholes and we know it. Take Mel, for example. He knows he's a loser who's never studied anything and will never do anything and that the farthest he can go in life is to direct a porno film. He knows he's a no-hoper. Your classmates, on the other hand—*our* classmates—are a bunch of assholes and they don't even know it. It's pretty sad to be an asshole and not realize it, don't you think?" I said nothing. "Who's Samuel?"

shit. "It's all organized," he said in his enchanting nasal timbre. "When the doors open, from here we can see the passage that leads to the escalators. As soon as the barriers are raised, Floyd'll go down and place lumps of shit on the floor, on the edges of the escalator, and on the handrails. When people start showing up, I'll take photos of their reactions, and then next month we'll display them in an experimental gallery in Las Palmas. What do you think of the idea?" he asked me while swallowing some gum. "It's disgusting," I said, without making a big thing of it. "Why?" he asked. "Christ, because it's shit! And shit is disgusting." "Eugenia," he said in a teacherly manner, "people only know how to deal with their own crap. There's nothing more intimate than shit. We want to share. We're altruists, our aim is to share." I'd never heard the word "altruist" before. A narrow strip of light appeared down below. Floyd set off with his cargo. Luis grabbed the camera and took a few snaps. The door to the Metro opened. It wasn't until 6:30 or 6:45 a.m. that commuters started to appear. The first, a thirty-year-old man who looked gay, stopped short when he encountered the shadowy substance. Luis pressed the button on the camera, and in close up, the man's face froze. He stood at the entrance to the subway, staring down incredulously at the sinuous pile of shit. He attempted to move forward, but immediately backed up. It seemed as though the repulsive stench were turning his stomach. Between one commuter and another, Luis told me many things. We talked a lot of nonsense. If I had to write down everything he said, those stories would lose their charm. Luis was fascinating to listen to because of the way he spoke, because of his furious gestures. One of the nicest series of photographs he took that morning was of a stray dog: nose to the ground, it began sniffing and turning in happy circles around the station. A little old lady made the sign of the cross and tried jumping onto the escalator. When she grabbed the handrails she gave a start, which nearly made her tumble over. The camera went click. The silhouette of the old lady—with a desolate expression on her face—vanished, descending into the bowels of the earth. The last photo showed a tragicomic image: a woman whose sandals were stuck in poo. When she realized what had happened, she sank to her knees and began to cry loudly and openly. Floyd fell asleep. Luis continued telling me stories. He talked to me about Brussels, France, and the Czech Republic. Stale and tired from being up all night, and somewhat drunk, I told him that I had a French grandfather who lived somewhere in the Andes. I told him about the embassy, the issue of being a third-generation descendant. "We'll always have Paris," I said, recalling the phrase from one of Daniel's favorite films, a cheesy movie in black and white that he normally watched in the early hours of the morning. "*Casablanca*," said Luis immediately. "What?" "*Casablanca*—the film. The phrase comes from that film." Years later, Vadier would tell me that people tend to fall in love over these kinds of details, or, put less delicately, over saying this kind of shit.

At 8:00 a.m. he accompanied me to Avenida Rómulo Gallegos. He called a cabdriver-friend of his, and we waited on the corner. He gave me three kisses goodbye: one on either cheek, and one on the forehead. "I had a great time with you. See you on Monday at school." "Yeah, me too. Bye." From the Metro station, we heard the cleaners hurling curses at the anonymous terrorists. The cab began moving.

Luis turned around and left quickly. With vague remorse, I turned on my cell phone. There were thirty-two missed calls from Jorge. The first few text messages showed a certain concern. After the sixth, he called me a whore. *Bitch, call me whatever time it is. Jorge went crazy. Nata.* I felt sleepy. I'd leave the melodrama for another time. When I arrived home, I went into my bedroom without brushing my teeth or taking off my clothes and threw myself on top of the bed.

TRAVEL PLAN

1

Luis Tévez had no sense in dealing with practical matters. A week after the "happening," when we finished class at the preparatory course, we had lunch together at the McDonald's in El Rosal. He asked me politely to take care of the order, because the cashier, a greasy-faced redhead, spooked him. Apparently, her ugliness left him speechless. "You don't have to say anything," I told him. "Just ask for some nuggets and a chicken-burger combo." "No, no, I can't. McDonald's makes me nervous." "Do you want to go to Burger King instead?" "No, no. They're all alike. Fast-food joints put me on edge. You order, please." He looked like a child who'd just seen the bogeyman.

Jorge, Gonzalo, and all the others who wanted to study engineering began a preparatory course at Central University on Saturdays, which meant they had to miss the last two hours of our useless workshop on communication and numeracy skills. Therefore I didn't need to invent any stories in order to go out and have lunch with Luis. As for my taking off with him the previous week, in the end I handled Jorge without any trouble. I turned the situation around to my advantage and made sure it was he who ended up asking for my forgiveness. I told him that, sure enough, I'd gone with Luis Tévez on his motorbike, but that all he did was give me a ride home. Before 1:00 a.m., I said, I switched off my cell phone and fell asleep. Jorge was suspicious at first, but later, after a few sloppy kisses, he seemed to buy it. Besides, I said to him, he'd broken my heart when he danced with that pathetic private-school bimbo. His bachata dance with her was the reason I took off. I remained cold and aloof toward him for a few hours until he apologized in a rather desperate way, feeding me lines from one of those Mexican soap operas they show on Televén.

Natalia laughed when I told her what had happened. "Did you fuck him?" she asked me. "No," I said in disgust. Lately, all Natalia ever thought about was sex. She found double meanings in even the most innocent of comments. Her aspirations in life seemed to have the graciousness of an erect dick. Her vocabulary was full of sexual references, and sex was all she ever talked about. At times she'd say things like "It smells of cum around here" just to make the nerdy girls, or more attractive guys, feel uncomfortable. To be honest, her overload of hormones embarrassed me. To me, she came across as cheap and tacky, unsophisticated. She couldn't get it into her head that I'd spent a whole night with Luis Tévez without even kissing him. Natalia had changed a lot. She wasn't like that before. She was much easier to deal with when we were younger. Since Gonzalo popped her cherry she'd become a real pain. Now she thought herself more womanly, more mature, more experienced than anyone else. Once, I made the mistake of telling her that I just couldn't wrap my head around the idea of having to take contraceptives. I told her that I'd never get used to popping a pill daily. After that, employing a whole bunch of gynecological jargon, she explained to me the benefits of taking the pill. She talked about different brands and pharmaceutical firms, about friends in common who had had various treatments. What annoyed me most were her pretensions, her overrated knowledge of the world. When Luis Tévez invited me to McDonald's, Natalia was standing right beside me. He hardly looked at her. I accepted. He said he'd wait for me in the parking lot. Once again, Natalia gave free rein to her horny imagination: "Bitch, if you don't fuck him, it'll piss me off. He's so beautiful. Don't worry, I'll tell Jorge that you weren't feeling well, that you came down with diarrhea, and that you went home." She gave me a kiss on the cheek and walked off, happy. Real happy.

"Have you found out anything about your grandfather?" The question took me by surprise. I'd almost forgotten my stupid plan to track him down. "No," I said. It was the truth. Alfonso had texted me the name of some woman and an address in a town called Altamira de Cáceres, but that's all I knew. "Tell me about your grandfather," he said to me as he removed the lettuce from his chicken burger. "I don't know what to tell you about him. I don't know him. According to my parents, I supposedly saw him once or twice." "And he's French?" "Yeah, he's French." "From what part?" "I don't know. I just know that he's French. That's where my surname, Blanc, comes from. His name's Laurent Blanc." "Laurent Blanc, like the soccer player!" "What soccer player?" "Laurent Blanc, man. France, '98! World Champion: Henry

sucks. Daniel didn't have many friends. He never mentioned Luis Tévez, nor was he a fan of the legendary students who'd been thrown out of school. "Daniel was gay, right?" "What the hell do you care?" I shot back. His questions hurt me. The only person I talked to about Daniel was myself. No one knew him. No one had the right to criticize him. But then, Luis's question didn't seem mean. It didn't come across as mocking or judgmental. After my outburst, I took a sip of my drink and then replied to him. Strangely, I felt comfortable doing it. He kept chewing on the end of his straw. An employee who was mopping the floor accidentally bumped my knee and apologized. "I liked that kid. You can't be gay in this country. Venezuela is a sort of alternative Middle Ages without priests or imperial projects. Total barbarity." I ignored his learned references. Besides, I didn't understand anything. "Do you remember a guy by the name of Albín?" I asked him. "I think so—a skinny little runt, Portuguese-looking?" I nodded. "He was Daniel's only friend. It was hard for me to talk to Daniel about his private life. We talked about other things. Albín had to leave the country, because his father signed some sort of decree. His family was sent packing from the Port of Carenero. This made Daniel really sad. Later, my stepdad, Beto, left, and my mother went crazy. A total mess." I still didn't have sufficient trust in Luis to talk about the pyromaniac. "It was one thing after another. He couldn't cope." "How did he end up doing it?" I stared at him with an odd mixture of hatred and need. I felt strange. I was treading on personal ground, far too personal. "He took some pills." I thought I'd burst into tears like a moron, but, weirdly, I controlled myself. I moistened my throat with a sip of Coke and some BBQ sauce. "That sucks! I once put a gun to my head." He chewed his burger and then, covering his mouth with his right hand, finished his story. "But I chickened out. I couldn't go through with it." Silence followed. He finished his Diet Coke but continued sucking on the straw. The melted water at the bottom made an unpleasant sound. He took the lid off the cup and began sucking on ice cubes. "So then, what'll you do about your grandfather? Will you go looking for him?" "I don't know. I wouldn't know where to start. I don't even know if the old guy's still alive." "The holidays start next week...What're your plans?" "What the hell, I suppose I'll end up going to Chichiriviche with Natalia. It's always the same." "Order two chocolate sundaes." He stood up and took out a scrunched-up bill from his pocket. "Go on, you do it. You know I hate ordering. My shout." I got up with a mixture of pleasure and annoyance. There were two others in the line. I went over my feelings from the last few minutes. I felt comfortable talking about Daniel. I hadn't even spoken to Doctor Fragachán about him. Not in that way. When I got back to the table, Luis appeared to be waiting for me, as if he'd thought up something nice to say and had been practicing it during my brief absence. "I'm going to Mérida on Easter Tuesday. Samuel Lauro lives in one of the residences at the University of the Andes. I need to talk to him. Come with me, and we'll look for your grandfather. I don't know where Altamira de Cáceres is, but if it's anywhere in the paramo, we could try. It might be cool. What do you say? Will you come?" I made no reply.

2

We took off on our trip in a shit box: a white, 1988 Fiat Fiorino. That old wreck—a type of small van—had a wobbly steering wheel that shook once the car hit 25 mph. Loud clunking sounds suggested there were several loose parts in the engine. The windshield was covered with a permanent film of dust; the grime gave the windows a tinted effect. The interior of the car smelled like chicken nuggets that had been left out in the sun. A 1980s-style blanket with red, purple, and yellow triangles covered the back seat. Hanging from the rearview mirror was a mobile with animal motifs: caimans, monkeys, chupacabras—those legendary cryptids—and a type of headless seal. The dashboard, almost entirely flaked off, revealed its cork padding. Above the glove compartment, whose lock had been substituted with a bit of wire, was a sticker of Our Lady Rosa Mystica. A heaviness hung in the air inside the spacious interior trunk; there the smell of chicken nuggets mixed with the smell of gasoline. A toolbox was wedged right behind my seat. Any sudden movements on my part and a Phillips screwdriver left its mark on my back. You'd have to be seventeen years old, have zero prospects for the future, a dysfunctional family, and a low threshold for boredom to agree to go on a road trip to the Andes under the conditions that I agreed to. I don't think Luis ever realized that our car was a piece of junk. He seemed happy and content. He was completely engrossed in "Visions of Johanna."

3

I didn't want to go to any hole or highland or moorland called Altamira de Cáceres to look for my grandfather, Laurent. That idea was no more than the vain hope of an insomniac. I'd never seen the old man before. According to Eugenia, he'd only ever visited the house two or three times.

The idea of having a French nationality was just a stupid fantasy, a corny idea, something to dream about. It was only when Caracas filled me with shit—something that happened quite often—that I remembered my childhood dream of finding this distant figure who could prove my ancestry.

Until then, the only places I'd ever been to were Chichiriviche, Puerto La Cruz, and Margarita. Beyond that, Venezuela was just a pistol-shaped map in a high school atlas. Regardless of my unpatriotic feelings, deep down I always knew that I would never get out of Caracas. I was convinced that it would be my eternal punishment. When Luis Tévez suggested I go with him to Mérida, and that we'd try to locate Laurent's town along the way, I didn't know what to say. I think my unintentionally rude comment was, "You're crazy." He mentioned something about some poetry readings, brought up the name of his idol, Samuel Lauro, and said something about certain performances. That morning I had a dull conversation with the ceiling and Mount Ávila.

At that time, Jorge appeared to have only one ambition: Chichiriviche. What a pain! Conscious of his mistake at Gonzalo's party, he put up with all my snubs with pathetic stoicism. It was awful. He didn't raise his voice once, gave me chocolates, and came up with convoluted arguments to convince me to join in "Operation Easter." He even went so far as to say that Señora Carmen—Natalia's mother—had said the holidays wouldn't be the same without me. A desperate man is capable of saying all kinds of stupid things. A number of times, I felt like telling him to go to hell, but the expression on his face, like that of a glue-sniffing street kid without his pot of strong glue nearby, filled me with a deep sense of pity.

Natalia started jumping around like crazy when I told her that Luis Tévez had invited me to go away with him. It was disgusting: she started acting like a dog who, after a week of being locked up inside, realizes its owner is taking out its leash and the keys to the house. "How fucking awesome, girl, you *have* to go…" She repeated a series of banalities and nonsense along those lines. I asked her to help me out with Jorge; even though I wasn't sure what I'd end up doing during the holidays, still I was convinced that I wouldn't go with them to Chichiriviche. At the same time, this strategy was a good ploy to sidestep Natalia's nosiness and Jorge's melodrama. I think Nata talked to him and told him that I was a bit depressed. "You have to give her some time, Jorge. She totally loves you. But right now, she just needs to be alone," she said to him tearfully. That snake in the grass knew how to lie.

Luis phoned me at my place and told me that he had found the route to Altamira de Cáceres. He said it was on the border between Barinas and Mérida, in a sort of Andean-type terrain. I said nothing. I don't like—I've never liked—making decisions. I've always trusted instinct more than logic. I went out for a walk to get some inspiration. A sudden desire to go on a shopping spree overcame me. I hit all the shopping malls: El Tolón, Sambil, and from Sambil on to San Ignacio. At one place, I bought a pair of really horrible sandals—retail therapy is the most effective kind of therapy. I killed some time in Esperanto, Tecniciencias, Nacho, Zara, and various other money pits. I even window-shopped at a place that specialized in granite kitchen countertops. Finally, having nothing left to do, I decided to have a bite at Evana's, the Chinese restaurant in the San Ignacio mall.

The spectacle commenced as soon as I reached the escalators: a housewives' uprising. By the looks of it, someone from the government—a female MP, from what I could gather—had gone out walking. A SWAT team of neighborhood women had recognized her and, armed with rolling pins, cheese graters, pots, blenders, and brooms, decided to teach her a lesson. Eugenia the dumbass got caught up in the middle of that confrontation. The MP's bodyguards, armed to the teeth, hurled insults and violently shoved some of the little ladies. What happened next turned into a real melee with pots and pans. I had never heard so many curses before. That was a show of utter contempt, with foaming at the mouth. I entered into a kind of trance. My ears were blocked. Reality changed tempo and began to unwind in slow motion. On reading the lips of a thirty-year-old woman crawling past in her car, I made out the word "whore"—a sincerely felt hatred in the Platonic sense. A fat woman carrying a brown bag, out of which protruded two baguettes, went past the point of no return. She advanced like a kamikaze, evaded the two distracted guards, and collared the angry MP, whose name, according to what I heard, was something like Dilia. It was impressive. The woman slapped her across the face with the baguettes and then squeezed her neck with the determination of a maniac. "I'm going to kill you, you bitch...D-i-e you c-u-n-t!" she said to her. A National Guard hit her in the stomach with a huge gun, and the woman didn't feel the impact. Several officials had to intervene, including the mall security guards, in order to get her off. I must admit, I found it funny—seeing the other pathetic wretch, with her filthy mop of red hair, choking on the ground, trying to take in

The seatbelt in the Fiorino wasn't working. The buckle meant to fasten me into the seat was covered in Scotch tape that had long since lost its grip. Our Lady Rosa Mystica eyed me with disdain and appeared to mock me. Luis had a cartoonish appearance. He gripped the steering wheel with repressed anxiety. The passenger-side mirror didn't exist. I had to tell him when to give way, or warn him when some asshole tried passing us on the right. We encountered our first accident just before the Los Ocumitos tunnel. We saw two National Guards; an ambulance; a van; a shape covered by a black blanket, from under which a hand with four fingers protruded; and, a few feet farther away, a Chevrolet Corsa overturned on the shoulder. Luis smacked the cassette deck, and once again, the tune came on. The harmonica announced the introduction of something called "Visions of Johanna."

5

All breakfasts are revolting. Between 6:00 and 11:00 in the morning, my body can only handle water or coffee. I've never gotten used to the virtues of eating breakfast: vitamins, iron, calcium, Frosties—it's possible that my body rejects all this crap in an act of self-defense. Doctor Fragachán said I had to watch my diet. He said my daily nutrient intake was insufficient and perhaps even carcinogenic. High levels of triglycerides and cholesterol suggested that I ought to avoid eating McDonald's for a while. Often, I forget to eat. However, when I do eat, I enjoy it. I tend to swallow without chewing. Natalia always said that I should be fat, that my face should be full of blackheads, and that somehow my body must just sweat out all the grease I consume with delight. Since I was a kid, breakfast has always been the most difficult meal: yoghurt doesn't appeal to me, the smell of scrambled eggs makes me nauseous, orange juice tastes like cat piss. The day we left for Mérida, Luis invited me to his place. I didn't know it was to have breakfast. Señora Aurora and the Maestro had prepared the national dish: pulled beef, black beans, rice, fried plantains, and arepas.

Luis explained to me that his mom's Toyota Yaris would spend the Easter at the repair shop. Apparently Señora Aurora had had an "incident" on Avenida Cota Mil and had tried to deal with the problem of overheating by herself. Luis's mother bought several bottles of water from a street-kid vendor and lifted up the hood like an experienced mechanic. Señora Aurora confused the radiator with the engine and tipped the three bottles of mineral water into where, hazily—in raised lettering—could be read "Oil." Naturally, the car wouldn't start. The incident threw a wrench into the holiday plans. Luis was frustrated. About two months ago, he told me, he'd arranged with her for the loan of the Yaris. Curiously, it was the Maestro who told him to go by the factory and talk to Garay. Two days before the trip, Luis asked me to accompany him to Los Ruices. That's where he'd meet with Garay, the watchman at his parents' company.

Garay was resourceful, Luis told me. He was Jack-of-all-trades at the factory: chauffeur, receptionist, chief of protocol, secretary, watchman, and manager. Luis's parents owned a textile factory. Apparently, they manufactured curtains, tablecloths, and bedspreads. As far as I could make out, the owner was Luis's father, but the administrator was Señora Aurora. I found it curious that it was that sponger, the Maestro, who suggested the alternative of Garay, but Luis's family was such an unusual bunch that I decided not to ask any questions or form an opinion. We met at the Metro station at Los Ruices. Luis was in a good mood. We talked nonsense, criticized everything in sight, and made fun of the world. We arrived at a sort of warehouse whose roller door was raised halfway. On entering, we saw a white car—a rust bucket—with its hood raised, held up by an umbrella. A short, dark man was stripping layers of sulfate buildup from an oxidized battery. "What's up, Garay. How're things?" "Li'l bro'! Fuckin' awesome! Your mom told me you was gonna take this wagon. I'll have it ready for you in a bit." That Fiorino looked like it had recently emerged from a scrapyard.

Pulled beef, black beans, fried plantains, arepas, and Malta soft drink. It was 9:00 in the morning: disgusting. The stench went right up my nose. I thought I was going to faint. It was like an episode of *True Blood* made in Venezuela. The Maestro was in his underwear. He was a really disagreeable person. Before stuffing it down his throat, he smothered his arepa in butter. Señora Aurora, on the other hand, sat by impassively and discreetly ate hers with cutlery. The Maestro's mustache was splattered with froth from his Malta. Luis was speaking with his mom. She asked questions, and he replied. The sordid ambience—quite sordid—was distracting. Several times Luis sputtered out, "But Mom," only to have Señora Aurora cut him short. "Don't be like that, Luis. I'm only asking you for a favor; besides, Jacquie is your aunt, the twins are your cousins."

"Aren't you going to eat, Eugenia?" Señora Aurora asked me, after witnessing my vain attempts at chewing a slice of bread with garlic. "I don't feel so well," I said. "I've got heartburn. Besides, this morning I ate a *cachito*." The events from that breakfast come back to me in flashes: snippets of conversation, lines of sauce dripping from the Maestro's arepa, the smell of fried plantains, burnt arepas. "Luis, are you taking that car to Mérida? Is it OK? Did you check the oil, the air in the tires?" Luis replied with his mouth full: "Garay said everything was OK." "Be careful, Luis. And don't speed. You know how dangerous that road is. Please remember what I asked you." Breakfast dragged on forever. Staying awake all night limited my ability to comprehend the world. I went over the ups and downs of that morning and asked whichever God there be—Catholic, Muslim, Jewish, Greek, or Indigenous—to extricate me, as quickly as possible, from that scene.

It had been easy to escape from my place. I told my mother that Natalia would come by early to meet me at the corner of our building. In fact, Nata gave me a ring at a quarter to eight. Without overdoing it, I gave Eugenia a hug and asked her for her blessing. "Be good," was all she said to me. A cab dropped me off at Luis's house. My level of nausea reached Code Red when I saw the sweet that Señora Aurora put down on the table in front of me: a mango jelly.

"Cassettes?" replied Luis's mother incredulously. "The truth is, I don't know. Enrique," she asked the Maestro, "do you know if there are any cassettes around?" The Maestro shook his head no. Naturally, the Fiorino didn't have a CD player. An argument about music preferences might have put an end to our trip. Luis was depressed about not being able to listen to music on the road. He didn't have any cassettes, nor did he know where to get some. After searching through the car, we found some of Garay's tapes in the glove compartment: Eddie Santiago; Las Chicas del Can; Wilfrido Vargas; José José; El Binomio de Oro; *Salsa, Volume III*; *Various Tracks in Spanish, Volume* 5; and Chayanne. "I refuse to listen to any of this shit," he said, putting his hands on his head, treating the situation as an irreparable tragedy. Later that night, after picking up the Fiorino, we talked on the phone. I said to him, "Don't give up. I'll bring my iPod and speakers." "Cool," he replied. Nevertheless, a prolonged silence ensued. "What have you got on your iPod?" he asked. "A bit of everything. Whatever you want." "Cool. Do you have anything by Nirvana?" "I think I've got one song. I'm not sure. Let me have a look." Like a moron, attempting to please him, I checked the contents and confirmed that I had something called, "The Man Who Sold the World." "What else have you got?" "I don't know, everything: El Canto del Loco, Camila, La Oreja de Van Gogh, Voz Veis, Nena Daconte, Juanes, Paulina Rubio." The bastard hung up on me. I called him back several times, but the answering machine just came on. Half an hour later, he called me back. He was hysterical. At first, I thought he was just joking, that he was parodying one of my lovers' quarrels with Jorge. It took me a while to realize that he was truly annoyed: "I've been throwing up for half an hour. How do you expect me to listen to that shit?" I dug in my heels. He remained inflexibly obstinate. He insulted me. I insulted him back. "Screw it, man! Go fuck yourself, you little wanker," I replied as a parting shot. This last volley shook him up. He changed his tone, his breathing returned to normal. "Do you have anything by the Rolling Stones?" "I don't know who those assholes are. No, I don't

he'd had the decency to put on a bathrobe that covered his belly and his boxers. Luis left the room, and I stayed behind checking through a shoebox. The old man spoke in whispers; his laugh suggested to me that he was saying something filthy. I made out: "If you're gonna fuck the chick, wrap it up…" He handed him something. "That girl's really hot, Luis! Well, make sure you fuck her good and proper, until it's coming out her ears. Have a great trip. God bless you." Damned sleazebag! I hated him with all my heart. I wanted to leave the room, grab a four-stringed cuatro from the hallway, and break it over his head. Filthy old bastard! Luis entered the room with a packet of condoms in his hand. He patted my shoulder sympathetically and said: "Don't take any notice of him. He's a nitwit. What can I say. I've been living with this troglodyte for more than two months." He seemed embarrassed. He was red in the face. Poor thing, I said to myself. It's not his fault he has to live with this clown. The momentary awkwardness was dispelled by a discovery. At the bottom of the shoebox I was holding in my hands, an orange shadow caught his attention. It was a cassette. Luis held the rectangular object in his hands and his face took on an expression of pure delight. On the cover was a photo of a shaggy-haired guy, young but clearly old as well, a somewhat classic look. Over his face I read the phrase *Blonde on Blonde*. "Who's that?" "Bob Dylan," he said slowly. After reading through the list of songs, he began to hyperventilate. "What's wrong?" I asked somewhat bored. "Nothing. 'Visions of Johanna,'" he repeated the name of the song two or three times: "'Visions of Johanna,' 'Visions of Johanna.' How cool!" We left Caracas at 9:50 a.m.

6

I'm not used to improvising. The few times I've done away with routine, an uncomfortable tingling feeling ran right through me. On the other hand, lying never causes me the slightest problem. It comes easy to me. When I told my mother that I'd be going to Chichiriviche with Natalia, I said it to avoid her questions and her brazen curiosity. I couldn't even answer most of those questions. An inner voice suggests I must have definitely had rocks in my head that Easter. Luis Tévez was a weird and wacky guy. He drove clutching the steering wheel as if his life depended on it, and every so often he pressed the rewind button on the radio-cassette player to listen—almost trancelike—to the song "Visions of Johanna." He behaved like an overly excited primary school kid playing on his Nintendo Wii. Nevertheless, despite his autism, he inspired me with the kind of trust that only my brother had managed. That inexpressible trust was what allowed me to be there. I left Caracas ignoring the route and the true motives for our adventure. For my part, it was assumed I needed to find my grandfather, although always present in my mind was the feeling that my search was madness. *Hi Laurent, I'm your granddaughter, Alfonso's daughter. Look, I need your passport and marriage certificate in order to prove our relationship.* I imagined that appeal to him with some skepticism. In an ideal world, the old man would probably fulfill my request, put a stamp on it, and seal off all my concerns, and, on top of that, wouldn't ask me any difficult questions. During the first part of the trip, I preferred not to think about Laurent. I suspected that, as usual, reality would once again turn its back on me. For his part, Luis was broken. In order to lower the window you had to tap it with the screwdriver a few times. "*Carmen*, a Venezuelan movie." "No, why would I watch that shit? I don't know what you're talking about." "Well, there's this National Guard in it, a useless drunk, a good-for-nothing lecher. My Uncle Germán is exactly the same as that piece of shit." A light drizzle enveloped the mountain. There was a lot of traffic. A 1970s Chevrolet Malibu with various air beds strapped to the roof passed by. In the window, darker than night, was a sign written in shoe polish that read: "From Barcelona to Nirgua." Luis asked me to light him a cigarette. When he took the Marlboro from my mouth, his fingers brushed my lips. It was a light caress, just a semblance. He didn't feel the jolt—nor did he flinch. He continued talking about his family and listening to Bob. "Now it seems," he said after blowing out some smoke, "that that bastard, Germán, is general of some division or other. Soon, they'll probably name him deputy minister. The other day he went on the talk show *Hello Mr. President*, clapping like a seal and pissing himself laughing. Dustin and Maikol are the worst. They both have Hummers. Now they're living the high life in Los Roques with some pieces of ass and some booze. A couple of creeps, who, just a few short years ago, not even God took any notice of." "Temporary Like Achilles" came on. "But my mom, who's an imbecile, made *majarete* and mango jelly and wants to send some to her sister, Jacqueline." I don't know why I had an attack of laughter. Luis laughed as well. Stupidity and laughter are closely related. "And then what? What's the plan?" "That's right," he said, "I didn't tell you. After that, we'll head on to San Carlos. We'll stay there for one night, tonight. There's going to be a party and a "happening" at Nairobi's cousin's place. All those badasses will be there: Mel, Vadier, Titina, Claire. And for tomorrow, I don't know, we'll decide in the morning. We could go directly to Mérida or spend a night in Barinas. It's all the same to me."

The uselessness of Luis Tévez never ceased to amaze me. His awkwardness was part of his charm. He didn't know how to do anything. People frightened him. Everything that involved interacting with others—including machines—caused him to fall apart. For example, he didn't know how to pump gas. He froze at the pump, staring at the meter. After leaving his place, we stopped at the Texaco in Las Mercedes. His complete immobility forced me to get out of the car, open the fuel cap, grab the pump, and start filling up the tank. When he saw me do it, he remained absorbed. After a few seconds, he rewarded my initiative with a lame: "Cool!" In those moments, I hated him. I felt like spitting at him. In the gas station, while he was waiting for the tank to be filled, I asked him to go to the convenience store to buy some Doritos, some sliced bread, and some deviled ham spread, just in case we got hungry. He had no idea how to do it. He went in and came right back out. He told me that it was too difficult for him. What's worse, he got all nervous, his forehead was perspiring, and his hands were shaking. "Nairobi asked me to bring two cases of beer and a bag of ice," he said to me with a look of distress, "but if we buy the ice now, it'll melt before we arrive. I'd prefer to buy it when we get there," he said. The thought of having to make another stop made his face crumble. "Will you buy it?" he asked me with fear in his voice. I didn't know whether to laugh or cry.

During the first few hours of the trip, there were various signs of Luis's uselessness. One of the most significant occurred after we passed the tollbooth. Besides Bob Dylan, another terrible sound was coming from the front of the car. At every turn, the engine started banging incessantly. It calmed down only when the speed was reduced and we maintained a straight course. It was unbearable. Luis said he didn't hear anything, that it was just an imaginary noise. When he couldn't pretend anymore, he told me that Garay had warned him: the car's noisy. "Dammit, Luis, that's not a noise! This shit won't even make it as far as—what's that place called...Victoria. Stop the car after that bend!" He lost control of the steering wheel and got real nervous. "Luis, stop! Let's see what it is." After numerous pleas, he decided to pull over. I asked him to open the hood and he told me he didn't know how to. Naturally, I had no idea either; but I figured that all that was required was some common sense. Luckily, it was simple. I reached under the driver's seat and pulled a lever. The rod that held up the hood was broken. I asked Luis to hold it up while I pretended to be a mechanic. He held on to it with a wild expression on his face, with nervous, bulging eyes. I ran my hand along the dusty gearbox and saw nothing strange. I don't know why I thought I might see something strange. I knew absolutely nothing about cars. Nevertheless, the noise was so bad I thought the cause would be obvious. On a second inspection, I discovered the problem: on top of a container filled with water, which I took to be the radiator, was a pair of pliers. I grabbed them and showed them to Luis. I remembered the day we picked up the Fiorino, when the Tévezes' watchman was cleaning the sulfate from the battery; various screwdrivers, hammers, and other tools had been scattered over the gearbox. "Garay, that dumbass, forgot this pair of pliers above the engine," I said. "Come on, Luis, let's go. I don't think there are any other problems." He lowered the hood down slowly, repeating the word "cool" to himself various times.

Luis likes taking photos. After breakfast at his place, he forced me to pose standing beside his mother and the Maestro. On the road, in the line before the tunnel, he pointed the lens at me and took various close-up shots. He had three cameras: a small digital one and two other bigger and more complicated ones. After our unexpected stop, he took a shot of me holding up Garay's pliers. It was intolerable. He took one shot after another; the clicking sounded intermittently, second after second. "Smile, Eugenia," he said, and I smiled. "Pull a face, Eugenia," and I pulled a face. "Pout like a whore, Eugenia." I raised my hand, and without removing the face I'd pulled, I gave him the finger. Luis took great shots. Next to his bedroom was an annex where he'd set up a kind of darkroom. It was a small passage filled with trays, machines, and pictures hung on pegs. That morning, after tossing several pairs of socks and underwear into a JanSport backpack, he showed the pictures to me. Some of them were familiar: a mangy looking dog walking in circles around a pile of shit; a woman squatting down with her hands on her head, observing a line of brown muck staining her sandals. One image in particular drew my attention: We were sitting down together, leaning against a balcony railing. I was asleep on Luis's shoulder. He appeared to be staring at a private and unimaginable horizon. Floyd must have taken the shot. I'm not usually vain, but in all truth, I was beautiful.

I don't know why, but I'm photogenic. "Do you like it?" he asked me while rummaging through a box filled with DVDs. "What?" "The photo." "Yeah, it's nice." "It's yours, a gift. When we get back, I'll blow it up and give it to you." "Thanks," I said to him out of usual politeness and without looking at him. It looked like a professional, artistic shot; it could have been a movie poster for one of those romantic comedies that opt for a happy ending in the most obvious way. "What are you doing?" I asked him. He opened a black bag and, one by one, pulled out various pirated DVDs. "I'm looking for Venezuelan movies," he replied. "Venezuelan movies?" "Yeah, we're organizing a 'happening' with Vadier and Floyd, a bonfire." I went over all the highs and lows of that eternal morning as we traveled down the highway. A huge green sign announced our arrival at Maracay. Something warned me that the meeting with Aunt Jacqueline and Uncle Germán would necessitate huge doses of tolerance. Luis swore loudly when we arrived at the house, and we realized there was a party going on.

BLUE LABEL

There are two types of vulgarity: contrived and natural. The world—my small world—was overrun with ingrained brutes and, at the same time, phony barbarians. It's one thing being vulgar by nature, and it's another putting it on. The Maestro, for example, was a typical case of a pretend philistine—a parody of a thug. Luis related a few anecdotes in which the disdain the Maestro received from others was regarded by that lowlife scum as a form of validation. Natalia—*that* Natalia—is another case in point of someone who gave the appearance of being tacky. She was probably the most stuck-up teenager in the whole of East Caracas, but for some obscure reason, she enjoyed concealing her arrogance behind vulgar words and phrases—mainly related to genitals. On the other hand, José Miguel, the fat guy who recited the ode to onanism at Titina's house, was naturally foulmouthed. He was just plain facetious. Without a doubt, José Miguel has to be one of the crudest guys I've ever met in my life, but his vulgarity—explicit and scatological—was never shocking; he was a wordsmith with insults. He had a remarkable ability to incorporate profanities, references to feces and bodily fluids, and other forms of offensive phallic imagery into a single speech. For their part, Luis's Uncle Germán and his cousins were a kind of hybrid. While vulgarity was deeply rooted in their primitive souls, at the same time they were commonplace, garden-variety scum.

The echoes of a merengue reached the street. Two National Guards armed with FAL rifles stood watch at the gate. Luis identified himself, and the taller of the two gorillas mumbled something into a walkie-talkie. Minutes later they opened the gate. The yard was filled with Hummers, Audis, and Explorer Vans. We were told to turn left and park beside the kitchen. The Fiorino went past that showcase of cars with pride and humility. As we moved away from the entrance, in the rearview mirror, I could see the guards laughing at our car. Dustin or Maikol came out to greet us. Maikol first and then Dustin, or vice versa. Being twins, they didn't just resemble one another physically; they were also identically stupid. The two clowns' first remarks were in reference to the Fiorino. They made friendly fun—mock friendly—of our "little ice cream van." Luis grabbed the bag of sweets and greeted them with forbearance. When he introduced me, one of them, Maikol or Dustin, not content with just extending his sweaty hand in greeting, gave me a kiss on the cheek, leaving behind an unpleasant trace of saliva. "Be patient, we'll leave soon," Luis whispered. We entered the house through the back door.

Uncle Germán's house was the archetype of the nouveau riche home. It was crass and tasteless. In the main living room there was a goat's head—or a deer or a guinea pig or I'm not sure what it was—mounted on the wall. The parquet floor was badly polished. Dog paws and the faint outlines of Nike trainers were imprinted all over its lacquered surface. The dining room furniture was a combination of marble and orange Formica. Beside the goat's head was a portrait of the president. The shoddiest-looking thing was the home theatre. One of the walls was almost entirely taken up by a flat-screen television. On every table, chair, and stool in the room were speakers whose leads were poorly concealed by a polka-dot carpet. Having to watch the crappy government talk shows in high definition must be an abomination, I said to myself. A fat army guy, splayed out on a wicker rocking chair, was asleep in front of the television. Outside in the yard, enthusiastic shouts could be heard.

Aunt Jacqueline was a scrawny woman with bags under her eyes. Her face looked like it had recently emerged from a washing machine without any fabric softener. She was wearing a sickly sweet perfume, a peach-scented fragrance that smelled like toilet cleaner. She greeted Luis with affection. She took his face between her hands and kissed him with heartfelt emotion. Meanwhile, Luis handed her the bag with the mango jelly and the *majarete*. There were a dozen people in the house. Mostly men. The younger ones were wearing khaki uniforms, but the older, paunchier ones were in Bermuda shorts. Aunt Jacqueline, to our dismay, suggested that we go out and join the young people standing around the pool. So we got to meet the twins' friends. Dustin's girlfriend—or Maikol's—looked like a model. She was unnaturally perfect: peroxide blonde, huge tits, symmetric ass.

At the edge of the pool were at least six chicks with perfect bodies and two stoned potheads. "Nephew! Nephew! How's it goin'?" cried out a deep voice from the dominoes table. Cap from Mission Ribas Remedial High School, T-shirt with the logo of the state oil company PDVSA, Hawaiian shorts, flip-flops—Luis was right: Uncle Germán was the epitome of gaudiness. The host, visibly drunk, got up and approached us. He put his hands on Luis's shoulders and hauled him off inside the house. For ten or fifteen minutes, I remained alone with the twins and their friends.

"So then, you're Luis's girlfriend," said Dustin or Maikol. "No. We're just friends." Smirks. "Friends?" Hee, hee, ha, ha, ho, ho: ridiculous little voices. One of the models gave Maikol, or perhaps Dustin, a disgusting smooch. "And where are the 'little friends' spending Easter?" "At Chichiriviche," I lied. "Hey, babe, I know you. You go to One Nightclub. I've seen you there, waiting in line," said one of the potheads, who stood up impulsively and tried twerking with me. Damned jerk! Ambushed from all sides by vulgarity, I resorted to a classic strategy: I asked where the bathroom was. On entering the house, I realized that someone else had arrived at the party. He was a tall, ordinary-looking old man, wearing jeans and T-shirt without a logo. Aunt Jacqueline greeted him with affection. From what I could gather, the visitor, Señor Ricardo, had spent a few years in Bogotá doing a Master's degree and had returned to Venezuela just two weeks previously. Noticing his presence, Uncle Germán forgot about Luis and toasted the new arrival extravagantly. "Ricky, bosom buddy, how's things?" "How's it going, Germán?" replied the other, evidently uncomfortable. "I just came by to say hello, that's all," he added. His dismissive gesture, his expression of disgust at all the commie crap, caught my attention. A corporal summoned Uncle Germán back to the dominoes table. As he was heading back, Aunt Jacqueline asked the visitor what he wanted to drink. Señor Ricardo said shyly that he'd like to have a small whisky, a Buchanan's on the rocks. At that moment, something strange happened: Uncle Germán, who still hadn't left the room, turned around brusquely. "What?" Aunt Jacqueline had a sudden fit of the giggles. The guest took his time realizing the question was directed at him. "A small whisky, Germán, a Buchanan's," he repeated. "Buchanan's!" said the other indignantly, and then roared with laughter. A group of enthusiastic corporals echoed him. "Here, in this house, we don't drink that shit. Here we drink Blue Label." "God!" whispered Luis, who only a few seconds ago had come and stood behind me. Señor Ricardo remained expressionless. "That's right, Ricky," continued Germán, "none of this going around drinking cheap stuff. In this house we drink Blue Label." Then he commanded authoritatively: "Jacquie, give our friend Ricardo a shot of Label." Aunt Jacqueline, with a servile smile, set out to comply with his order. However, there was only a tiny amount of amber fluid left in the bottle on top of the table. Dustin—or probably Maikol—randomly entered the room. Germán saw the empty bottle and cursed loudly. Then he called out to the twin passing by: "Hey, my boy, bring us a couple of bottles of whisky from the pantry." Aunt Jacqueline asked Luis to accompany his cousin. "Please, wherever you go, don't leave me alone," I said to him desperately.

The pantry was at the rear of the kitchen. The door, which was blocked by the Fiorino, could barely be opened.

On entering the pantry we saw at least twenty-two cases of whisky stacked one on top of another—Johnnie Walker Blue Label. There were also boxes of Wii systems, PlayStations, televisions, boat motors, and Heineken beer. "Dude, if you wanna stay, we're gonna throw an awesome party tonight. The oldies are goin' to La Orchila, and the house'll be all ours. There'll be music and some ass, it'll be fuckin' awesome. You should come." I felt my knuckles go white. "Yeah, sure thing, Dustin. Let me just call some friends and see what they've got lined up." "Bring your friends, don't let that stop you," replied Dustin. The twin grabbed three bottles, and we went out into the yard. As we were heading back to the living room, we bumped into the sweet aunt. "Aunt Jacquie, we're leaving now, some of our friends are waiting for us," said Luis with a childish expression on his face. "Oh, Luisito, but you can't leave without having eaten. I just talked to your mom and told her that you'd be having lunch here. The barbecue will be ready in twenty minutes."

"Dammit, dammit, dammit!" Luis chanted in a low voice. We were sitting alone at one of the tables. I told him not to worry. I tried to distract him with stories about school, but a display of grotesquery rendered all my efforts futile: the army guy splayed out asleep on the rocking chair in front of the television threw up on himself, barely moving. Then, after waking up and breathing in the sour smell of his vomit, he ordered a couple of the corporals to wipe clean his epaulettes. Aunt Jacqueline brought us some cookies and then grilled Luis about family matters. "Tell me, Luisito, how's Armando? What have you heard about him?" "He's good, he's fine," Luis replied without enthusiasm. "How lovely of Aurora to send me some of her sweets. Why don't you go out to the pool and enjoy yourselves with the other young people?" Luis, with a blank look on his face, told her that I wasn't feeling well. Aunt Jacqueline looked at me with pity. "Sciatica," I said with a resigned expression. Then she asked Luis about the Maestro, about yoga, about some pastry-cooking courses, and about various other things that I've forgotten about. After that, Dustin and Maikol called out that the barbecue was ready.

Fortunately, they sat us beside Señor Ricardo. Dustin, Maikol, and their gang sat up front. At the head of the table was Uncle Germán. The corporals acted as waiters. Luis and Ricardo conversed in low voices. I managed to catch that he'd known Luis's parents a long time. Uncle Germán was very drunk. The twins were talking loudly. Suddenly, silence filled the room. With a forced smile, Germán downed a glass of whisky and, banging his fists on the table twice, asked: "Listen here, Luisito: That conspirator you have for a father—where's he hiding out? What sewer is Armando Tévez holed up in?" The other army guys laughed at the joke. The twins remained silent. I put down my knife and fork. I didn't know which way to look, nor what to do. I thought that Luis might blow his top. Strangely, he remained calm. "In Costa Rica, Germán," he replied without flinching. "He had no choice: they caught him and he had to leave." Uncomfortable laughter. "Listen, Luis, I hope it's clear to you that, in this house, we're on the side of the Revolution." "Yeah, I know, Uncle, no sweat, don't worry." Germán's false smile faded, his eyes filled with rage. Aunt Jacqueline, terrified, tried to smooth things over and remarked on the wholesomeness of the guacamole. Silence resumed. Luis unabashedly let out a sardonic laugh: "Chill out, Uncle, it's clear to me that this country's in the hands of the rabble." Oh my fucking God, I said to myself, they're going to kill us right here, put us in jail. Luis continued: "My father has adopted the policy of Doña Florinda. Do you know who I'm talking about? The character played by Florinda Meza in *El chavo del ocho*. Have you seen the show?" Uncle Germán banged his fists on the table again. Mr. Ricardo laughed quietly. "Doña Florinda always tried to steer clear of what she called 'the rabble.' There's a famous scene in that series, which I'm not sure if you'll remember…" Luis cut a slice of yuca, speared it with his fork, and swallowed it. With his mouth full, he continued with his account: "Doña Florinda couldn't stand Don Ramón, whom she considered a scumbag; whenever she could, she'd try to humiliate him. One day, when she saw Don Ramón bothering her son, Kiko, she approached Don Ramón and gave him two slaps. Then she said: 'Come along, Kiko, let's not associate with that lowlife.'" Slowly, pausing after each syllable, Luis added: "To which Kiko parroted: 'Lowlife, lowlife.'" Luis ended his account by blowing a raspberry. Uncle Germán stood up and knocked the plates off the table, sending them crashing to the floor.

"Don't fuck with me; show my family some respect! I won't stand for this bullshit, you little brats!" We politely left the table. Uncle Germán accused us of assaulting authority and ordered one of the fearless corporals to lock us up. Aunt Jacqueline cried out and gave a counter order. Señor Ricardo asked everyone to remain calm and tried to placate the twins, who threatened to kick our asses. When we got to the kitchen, in order to avoid an attack, we made a run for it. "*Golpista*, man, that's what your father is, a traitor!" "Arrogant shits, fucking oligarchs!" "Germán, please calm down," said a woman's voice. We went out into the yard, unable to control our hacking laughter. The row inside the house continued, but all we could hear from outside were isolated curses and insults. We climbed into the Fiorino. Luis started it up immediately. He'd barely driven ten feet when he slammed on the brakes. "Wait for me here!" he said excitedly. He opened the door and ran toward the back of the house. In the rearview mirror I saw him enter the pantry. As if we had been a couple of fugitives who, after spending years in prison together, understood each other's craft well, I gathered his intent. I turned around in my seat and, from inside, opened the back door. First pit stop, one box; second pit stop, another box; third pit stop, one more box. We could hear the twins' aggressive voices only a few feet away. Luis flung himself into the back of the Fiorino with an awkward jump, pulled the door shut behind him, and threw me the keys. "Drive," he said euphorically. Everything happened quickly. Suddenly, the steering wheel was in my hands. I stepped on the gas and crossed the parking lot. During the getaway, I swiped the bumper of an Explorer Van. Fortunately, the sentry box was empty. (Later on, Luis told me that he saw one of the National Guards pissing behind a palm tree. The other guard wasn't there.) I accelerated, and three blocks later on, I had to stop because I was out of breath. At the gas station just before the Tapa-Tapa tollbooth, we took stock of our loot. We'd stolen twenty-four bottles of whisky.

SAN CARLOS

1

Laughter and silence, in counterpoint, became the highway. The road was surrounded by green hills and dotted with smokestacks. The soundtrack of the landscape was performed by Bob Dylan. Lake Valencia, for example—that remote cesspool—is a memory that presses "Play" on "Rainy Day Woman." The memories are assembled out of bits and pieces: the breeze on my face, the unbearable smell of chicken nuggets, Luis's earnest, out-of-tune singing. Green signs announced the names of places I'd never heard of before. I knew of Valencia. I'd also heard of Barquisimeto. The other names were just hazy hieroglyphics. Our final burst of laughter, inspired by our wanton act of plunder, resulted in a long stretch of silence. "Where's San Carlos?" I asked. "In Cojedes. It's the capital." "And what's in San Carlos?" "Nothing," he replied. "And what's in Cojedes?" "Nothing." "I've never been to Cojedes." "Me either." "What a bleak and desolate place this is!" I said to him while staring at the dreary horizon. My hair fluttered around my temple. The song "Pledging My Time" began to play. "It's one of those ghost towns that probably has a legendary past." "A legendary past?" I hadn't shaken off the absurd habit of responding to him with questions. At our school, Luis was something more than just different. He had a sophisticated vocabulary; he used words that, although familiar, would never have occurred to me to use. Besides, he knew things: geography, history, literature. He seemed to know all that stuff you're supposed to learn for pointless exams, and what's even stranger, he found it enjoyable. "That jerk Bolívar," he said. "What?" "I reckon Bolívar passed through San Carlos and kicked some ass. That's the city's main claim to fame." "I don't know, I've got no idea." "Bolívar was a shameless prick," he went on. He was talking to himself. I knew nothing about history; mention of Bolívar's name gave me hives. "The dude stopped in San Carlos and gave the Spanish hell. Monteverde, the leader of the Spanish forces, was the real deal, but he fled to Puerto Cabello. The problem of independence could've been resolved that day. Bolívar simply had to attack the port and crush the jerk. Monteverde was finished. He didn't have an army, he didn't have arms, everyone avoided him. History would've been different if Bolívar had attacked Puerto Cabello, but no...the total jerk went to Caracas instead. He allowed the enemy to regroup, to arm themselves, to get reinforcements from Spain, to enlist that opportunist Boves, and to win territories—all because he wanted to fuck some chicks, get pissed, and have his ass kissed. Do you know Santiago Mariño?" The question brought to mind memories of past vacations. "I think it's the name of a street in Margarita," I replied, bored and unsure. "He was—how can I put it—the

his face, was holding a wooden spoon while keeping an eye on the temperature of the soup. Nairobi, accompanied by a fat brown-haired woman—the owner of the house—was dragging a crate of beer. Luis introduced me to various groups of friendly drunks. They seemed older—twenty-something, and some who were even thirty. I felt comfortable in that house of strangers. Normally, I don't like meeting people. When I'm surrounded by strangers, an all-pervasive shyness tends to come over me. In that house in San Carlos, making small talk with people I barely knew, I didn't feel any pressure. Natalia texted me obscene questions, which prompted me to turn off my cell phone. Luis was generous with his hospitality. He crossed through the house, regaling everyone with a bottle of whisky. There were cheers and sloppy thanks all around. José Miguel started to cry. He cradled his bottle like a baby, whispering lullabies to it and kissing the label. Mel immediately opened his gift. Then he knocked back a shot of whisky that burned his throat. Nairobi brought out some plastic cups and distributed them among the festive crowd. The last to arrive was Floyd. He looked like such a blob! Luis handed him a bottle. Floyd mentioned that he had everything ready for the "happening."

"Why do you know all this stuff? What kind of strange weirdo are you?" I'd asked him on the road after he expounded his historical views. "What stuff? What are you talking about?" "All that stuff! History, Bolívar, Mariño, and whatnot." "I don't know. I suppose I must've read about it at home at one time or another." "Don't you find it annoying?" "No, it's fun. The history of Venezuela is really entertaining." "I don't know. I've never liked history." "History the way it's taught at school is a piece of crap, but believe me, if you learn it on your own, it's a real trip. All of those heroes were clowns"— song: "I Want You"— "My father had a huge library with lots of history books." "Your father? Armando?" His expression suddenly changed. He took his eyes off the road and looked at me curiously. Then, after a few seconds, his eyes returned to the road. "Yeah, Armando." "And where did the Maestro come from, is he your stepdad?" "No, the Maestro's my mom and dad's best friend." "That's a bit weird." "Yeah, my family's weird. Armando's in Costa Rica, because he was caught allegedly financing an 'attempt.' The day before he left, Floyd and I had to help him wipe a few hard drives and laptops. This'll make you laugh: my mom's been my dad's first, second, and third wife. It's crazy, they can't stand each other, but they don't know how to live apart. They get together, get married, get divorced, and then do it all over again. Besides which, they think of themselves as twenty-year-olds and act like hippies; now they believe in free love and sleep with their friends, they smoke weed and listen to Led Zeppelin. A few months ago, while I was in Belgium, my mom started taking yoga classes and traditional pastry-cooking courses. Armando's a good guy, he's a bit crazy, but most of what I know I owe to him. When I was a kid he used to read me horror stories and crime novels. And what about your parents?" he suddenly asked. I responded with an abrupt laugh. I took a while in replying. I wasn't expecting that difficult question. "My mom's crazy, my dad's even crazier." "Who's Laurent's kid, him or her?" "Him." "He must be a really cool guy." "No, believe me he isn't. He's not worth shit." "Dammit, Eugenia, sure, parents fuck things up, but underneath it all they're just people. Somehow they're always there." "Alfonso's never been there." I was calm, lost in the scenery. My words lacked emotion and depth. A Llanopetrol gas station sign brought back sad memories. Once again, Alfonso's name was engulfed in fuel. "Has your dad ever wanted to kill you?" I asked him. Luis shrugged his shoulders. "I suppose when I was a kid he wanted to kick my butt a few times, but I reckon that's normal," he replied. If I'd thought about it, I wouldn't have asked him. It was an instinctive question. I'd never talked about any of this before. "No. I'm serious. Has your father ever wanted to kill you?"

Floyd was dragging a huge puppet, a cardboard cutout with piñata tassels that appeared to represent a short, fat, older man. The puppet was wearing thick horn-rimmed glasses and a red T-shirt. Luis and Mel were carrying black bags. "Hi," said a clear and friendly voice. It was Vadier Hernández. "Hi, how are you?" I replied, smiling. "You're?" "Eugenia," I said. "Luis's girlfriend?" "No, well, I'm not sure." We laughed in unison like a pair of idiots. After opening the bags, Mel began taking out various pirated movies, one by one. "What are they doing?" I asked. Vadier poured himself a shot of Blue Label and said: "We're having a 'happening.'" Floyd dragged the puppet into the middle of the patio and hung it up on a tree. Then he put several bricks beneath the surrogate Judas. Nairobi was chopping some wood with an ax. "We're making a bonfire of Venezuelan films. We're gonna burn that shit as a sign of protest," explained Vadier. "Who's the puppet?" "The film director Román Chalbaud."

"My mom asked him to leave home, she was already seeing Beto," I told him on the road. "My father, Alfonso, was staying in the apartment of a friend who was on vacation in

Miami. He had many problems with my mom. He disappeared for about three or four months. Suddenly, after an attack of remorse, he asked to see us. He said that he wanted to talk to me and Daniel. Feeling pressured after listening to one of Eugenia's little speeches, we reluctantly agreed to go see him after school. It was awful, Luis. He welcomed us with some cold Chinese takeout. After giving us a rundown on the downside of divorce, he showed us his terrible films and appearances in commercials from the nineties." "Was your dad an actor?" "He was never an actor. He was a kind of extra—an *extra* extra. We spent the afternoon at his place. He told us that he loved us, that he missed us, that Eugenia was a piece of shit. At around six or so, we decided to leave. The melodrama of that goodbye was appalling. One block from his building, I realized that I'd forgotten my folder. I needed that fucking folder because there was some homework in it that I had to submit the following day. Daniel kicked up a stink, said how dare I forget my folder, he was really annoyed with me. I told him to stop being hysterical and to wait for me. I'd go back to Alfonso's place alone and get the folder. Daniel hated my dad; they didn't get along at all. Alfonso was really cruel toward Dani. It all happened when I returned to the apartment."

I played bowls for the first time in my life. It was fun. I formed the Green Team with Claire. The burgundy-colored balls belonged to Titina and José Miguel. I bowled close to the jack, and Claire delivered dead bowls—this was the jargon Luis used to describe our actions. I'd never drunk whisky before either. That expensive Blue Label whisky was strong. It burned the back of my throat like acid. There were at least twelve bottles scattered around the patio tables.

to that sweetly pathetic scene. My saliva stung. My throat clenched, as if to close around my words. "When I returned to the apartment, Alfonso had emptied a can of gas over himself. He had a cigarette lighter in his hand and was about to set himself alight. He told me that his life was shit, and that he wanted to kill himself. I didn't stop him. I thought it was just another one of his bad acts, some sort of mad skit. I just wanted to grab my folder and get the hell out of there. Without realizing it, he came over to where I was standing and hugged me forcefully. He told me that he was going to hell and that he wanted me to go with him. He grabbed a can of that shit. He doused me with gas from head to toe. I went crazy, I started kicking and cursing him. In the end, I managed to bite his wrist and break free. My mouth filled with that disgusting liquid, but luckily, I managed to grab the lighter off him. If Daniel hadn't returned, I don't know what might have happened. Alfonso was crazy. He started rambling, insulting my mother, saying that his father was a disgrace, his son was a faggot, and his wife was a whore. Dani transformed. I'd never seen him get so angry before. Who knows where he summoned the strength from to confront him? They tumbled onto the floor, grappling, punching, and kicking each other hard. Daniel grabbed him around the throat. I thought he was going to kill him. 'Daniel, let's get out of here,' I said. 'Daniel, let's go,' I said much stronger. 'Daniel!' I shouted. Finally, he let go. Alfonso started to cry. 'I don't want them to put you in prison because of this piece of shit,' I said. I grabbed my brother, and we left. We never said anything about it to Eugenia. I never saw my father after that, until about a month ago, more or less, when he arranged to meet me in a hooker's bar to tell me that my grandfather, Laurent Blanc, lived in a town called Altamira de Cáceres."

New guests arrived. Each of them was regaled with a bottle of Blue Label. "Dammit, how annoying, the Patriot's come," Luis said to me, indicating one of the newly-arriveds. "Keep away from him, he's a real pain in the ass." To my surprise, before he went off, he kissed the top of my head. The hour of the "happening" arrived. Vadier was the MC. He was radiant, commanding. He looked nothing like the bum who, a few weeks previously, had smoked a curry joint at Titina's house. Luis explained to me that Vadier was "tri-polar." His friends called him "Sybil" in reference to an old film. They said he had multiple personalities that alternated according to the phases of the moon. Titina read aloud a manifesto, inviting all those present to participate in the burning of Venezuelan films. "Román Chalbaud will burn in the circle of mediocrity," she said in conclusion. "Here," Luis said, handing me a copy of *Secuestro express*, "I imagine you've seen it." "Yeah, I've seen it. What do I do with it?" I asked him in a low voice. Nairobi asked for silence. "I'll explain." Vadier was the Grand Inquisitor. He grabbed a black cover with red letters and began a sermon: "I chuck this overrated piece of garbage titled *Cangrejo* into the fire. May this farce forever vanish from this earth." The film burned beneath the puppet. Then Titina jumped into the ring. Floyd ran around taking photos of everything. Titina threw *Cuchillos de fuego* into the fire. She took out a sheet of paper from her pocket and read: "May this useless footage disappear forever. Chalbaud must be condemned for crimes against humanity. When I lost two hours of my life watching this garbage, my human rights were violated."

And, in that way, one after another, all of that man's films were burned: Pelolindo, *La gata borracha*; José Miguel, *Pandemonium*, etcetera. The fire intensified. The puppet caught fire. The films of various other guys such as Diego Rísquez, Solveig Hoogesteijn, Carlos Oteyza, and Óscar Lucien were also burned. Nairobi's speech was particularly funny: "I chuck Clemente de la Cerda's films into the fire," she said. "We don't want any more idealized, romanticized shanty towns, hell no! Are the passions and desires of sociopaths the only ones that count in this shithole of a country?" Applause and cheers. A protocol began in which all those present participated. Everyone had to throw a film into the fire and say a few words. The puppet gave off a black and orange smoke. The one called the Patriot burned *Elipsis*. An old balding man, known as the Professor, burned two DVDs by someone called Carlos Azpúrua. When it came to my turn I walked up to the fire. I had *Secuestro express* in my hands. Luis had whispered the speech to me minutes before: "I burn this crappy piece of second-rate morality and kind-hearted thugs." I forgot the rest of it. I threw the DVD into the pit of fire.

Luis pulled up in front of a store selling goats. He stared at me blankly. My confession had sought his tenderness or his pity, but his face remained impassive. "That sucks!" was the only thing he said. He squeezed my hand and then let go of it. In accordance with romantic traditions, I thought that he'd hug me and then, compelled by circumstances, we'd kiss for the first time. But none of that happened. "I'm hungry," he said after a few moments of icy silence. "With all of the uproar that Germán caused, it only gave me time to chew on half a yuca. Get me some of that deviled ham and sliced bread that we bought in Caracas." Then he smiled.

I wanted to get out of the car, slam the door, and insult him like a little kid. But I couldn't do it. He took my hand, held if for a few seconds, and tickled my palm with his fingers. "These things happen, Princess, life's shit!" "What did you just say?" I asked, indignant. "What did you just call me?" I snapped. He laughed. "Princess!" he said. "That's what my friends nicknamed you. Claire or Titina, I don't know which one, decided to call you Princess." "What a lousy nickname; I'd rather they called me—I don't know—the name of some animal or whatever else less ridiculous." "You made a good impression. I think they discussed calling you Cutie Pie, but in the end they were kind to you and settled on Princess." "How awful!" I said. Silence fell. Bob Dylan again. "Dammit, Luis, this guy Dylan is really great, but I can't stand him anymore." "Don't worry. In less than half an hour we'll arrive in San Carlos."

3

I don't know how to relate to other women. I understand female friendships as a type of transaction. I can't stand competitiveness or silent envy. In general, my best friends have been men. With women I tend to sign a contract—a dodgy contract with qualifying periods and small, miniscule print. All my friendships from school faded. Eventually, some of those old friends appear on social media sites, flaunting kids and husbands in their profile pictures. I suffer the stigma of the outsider: everyone thinks I'm an alien. The coolest chick I've ever known in my life has been Titina Barca. There was very little I was able to share with her, but our few conversations always exhibited a genuine ease without prejudice.

The soup was tasteless. Limp pepper strips and onion floating in dirty water. The yuca was hard and the potatoes— or celery or taro, they're all the same—had green tints. Despite my disgust I ate two bowls. My stomach was weak, and my esophagus was burning. The fiery whisky rendered my body useless. Sliced bread and deviled ham, stashed in the Fiat, served as a side dish. Food brought on tiredness. José Miguel fell asleep on the table. Vadier underwent a metamorphosis and impulsively began running through the house, shouting that life was repetitive. The one called the Patriot was making corny speeches, inviting the card players to join the student union of which he was the sports delegate. Many of the drunks at San Carlos were university students, and almost all of them—at one time or another—had attended our high school. Claire, for example, was studying tourism; Pelolindo, second-year law; Nairobi, according to what I'd been told, studied visual arts. After the soup, battling lethargy, Titina brought out a case of beer. The guys stayed inside the house. Some played dominoes, others watched porn, played Ouija, or discussed future "happenings." I went out onto the patio. Nairobi was lying on the ground, holding a guitar. Her cousin, the fat brown-haired woman, lay with her head on Nairobi's shoulder. Titina was squatting down, smoking a joint. With a friendly gesture, she invited me to join them.

"I don't do shit," she replied when I asked her what she was studying. "I don't do a damn thing," she added with a smile. I'd never met anyone I could relate to so much. She lacked occupation and didn't care. Titina was a pleasing reflection, a copy in high resolution of my aspirations. Nairobi strummed the guitar. We sang a few of Shakira's old songs. We stopped the songs halfway through, changing the words and the melodies. Inside the house, at a distance, I could make out Luis in a fierce discussion with the Patriot. His hostile gestures caught my attention. "Do you like him?" asked Titina, blowing smoke near my face. "Yeah," I shrugged, "whatever." Titina's reply was interrupted by a beam of light. "Goddammit!" shouted Nairobi. Floyd's camera discharged a couple of flashes. "Floyd, stop being so annoying, get out of here, don't fuck around so much." Indifferent to the complaint, the albino took another shot. He asked us to smile, and, blinded by the flashes, we smiled like a bunch of morons. He thanked us and left. "That kid looks like an apparition!" said Nairobi's cousin. "That weirdo's a ghost, no one knows where he came from," Nairobi replied. "He sure is an ugly fucker!" I said. "Christ, Titina, where did this guy come from? He's Luis's neighbor, isn't he?" Nairobi asked. Titina inhaled the joint and said nothing. Nairobi related a funny story about him: "The other day I ran into him at the San Ignacio mall. I was there with someone from school, and the freak came up and said hi. The guy I was with invited me to a party in Miranda. Floyd came up to me just as he was giving me the address. I greeted him and then just ignored him. Well, bitch, the following day when I was at that party, the ghost appeared. On the intercom he said that I'd invited him. He's got some balls!" A strident screech interrupted the tale.

"You need to jerk off, you need to jerk off!" shouted José Miguel. The fatty, with the remains of vegetables in his incipient goatee, was running through the house, imploring everyone to masturbate. Mel, who was getting some ice, told us that José had argued with Claire. Claire reproached him for the macho character of his poetry. She told him his *peomas* were vulgar and misogynistic. José Miguel snapped back that she'd never understand the sublime significance of a good wank. Claire launched into a harangue. José Miguel, like a madman, started running around the patio. Suddenly, a string of insults was heard coming from the kitchen. Mel explained that Pelolindo, Luis, and the other rats were playing Ouija. "Why the fuck are they cursing?" Nairobi asked, while scratching her belly. "They're invoking the spirits of bad poets to insult them," said Mel. "A short while ago we invoked Francisco Lazo Martí and let him have it." Then Mel parodied one of his poems: "'It's time you came back / It's time you returned / No more shall you adorn / Your manly chest / With insane loves feasts / With myrtle and rose and pale jasmines.' Christ, what crap! We summoned the spirit of that son of a bitch and asked him for an explanation. He didn't reply. Then Luis started shouting, 'Sad excuse for a poet.'"

"Why are they doing these things?" I asked Titina when Mel left. Nairobi's cousin remained asleep on the ground. Nairobi had gone to the bathroom. Titina was playing with my hair and drinking beer. "What things?" She had a gentle voice, pleasant and inviting. "These crazy things," I said. "Performances, "happenings," burning movies, filling up the Metro with shit." Titina let out a short guffaw. "They're just things they do: Luis, Mel, Samuel." "Do you know that guy Samuel?" She looked me straight in the eyes with a vague expression. She nodded, yes. "A moron," she added. "Luis admires him," I said to her in a low voice. "Luis doesn't know him. Samuel Lauro's a thirty-year-old poor devil who makes photocopies in one of the faculties at the University of the Andes. The rest is all bullshit."

"The Patriot threw up," said Nairobi. "Motherfucker!" the cousin cried out in her dream from the ground. Nairobi came back to the patio, swearing repeatedly under her breath. "Dammit, the whole bathroom is covered in vomit, the basin, the toilet bowl, the towels. The bastard's fallen asleep in the shower." Appalled by the patriotic stench, the spiritualists ran outside and sat around the card table. Titina got up and put on a CD by the Beatles. I haven't described Nairobi with sufficient thoroughness. That chick is—was—incredible. I've known few women with such a bold, assured, engaging, and authentic femininity. Initial accounts of her took the form of rumor. To us schoolgirls she was a heroine. Natalia would recount anecdotes about her, offering them up as exemplary precepts. At one point, Nairobi had a boyfriend. Apparently he was a withdrawn and aggressive type, a friend since primary school. The guy was annoying, unbearable, a real jealous type, besides which—according to Nairobi—he had the added disadvantage of being a bad fuck. Nairobi's little boyfriend had gotten real close to her mom. He'd go over to their place in the evenings, and on weekends he'd show up with bags of croissants for breakfast. Nairobi decided to end it with him. The guy thought he deserved another chance. He followed her around after school and spent the afternoons making chitchat with her mom. A few months previously, Natalia had told me how it all turned out. Titina and Nairobi were playing Wii at Nairobi's place. Out in the hall, the dimwit of a boyfriend was criticizing the government with the mom. Just before midnight, the little boyfriend decided to leave. He went into the room to say goodbye. He made a sad-sack face and put on the voice of a deaf-mute: "Bye, Titina, be good. Bye,

reached the bowls court. "What?" "A little while ago, when I asked you what you were studying, you told me that you weren't doing shit. I was impressed that it didn't seem to bother you. I'm going to graduate soon and, in truth, I don't wanna do a fucking thing. I don't know what I want to do, nothing interests me, but I can't sleep because of it. I suppose you've gotta do something. I don't know." She tossed a few broken branches in the direction of the bush. "It's fucked, that's the truth. I exaggerated when I told you that I wasn't doing anything. Yeah, I've done a few things. Last year, I finished high school in an adult-education program. Then, through a contact, I got accepted into Santa María University, but I became fed up. Law school is crap. After that, I studied Business Admin at Humboldt University. That has got to be one of the shittiest places on this planet. I met a lot of morons there. You think you've met morons until you go to Humboldt. But, what the hell, sometimes I help the guys from the Reverón Art Institute with some of their events. My old man died about four years ago and left me a bit of dough. Either way, what's one supposed to do!" She revealed things which it would never have occurred to me—not even in a million years—to talk about with Natalia. My "best friend" boasts that title only out of habit and unavoidable coexistence. "Don't worry so much about it, Eugenia, just chill. Things have a way of working out on their own. All you have to do is believe that everything will be fine. That's not just some New Age bullshit, don't get me wrong, it's just knowing that things will turn out somehow. Can I tell you something?" We began sorting the bowls and placing them in a bag. "About two years ago, these little assholes started saying that I'd had my tits done.

People talk a lot of shit. The truth? I must be real drunk to be telling you this stuff. I've never talked about it with anyone, not even with Nairobi. Luis is the only one who, more or less, knows something." She dropped the bag a few steps away and lit a cigarette. "A few months prior to that, I was diagnosed with cancer. A lump came out here"— she placed her hand on her chest —"and they had to operate. I was in senior year at high school. That's the reason I had to leave school. Some pathetic asshole invented the story that I sucked off some professor's dick, total bullshit. People talk pure shit." I didn't know what to say. Her revelation was unexpected and hard to come to grips with. My first question was prompted by political correctness: "And how are you now, how are things going?" What an idiotic question! I said to myself. "Fine," she replied calmly. "My left tit's fake. None of these assholes know that. Well, Luis does, of course. But I'm OK. I'll tell you one thing though: I'm not gonna let trivial things bother me. When life wants to, it fucks you over; while it's not fucking you over, the best thing to do is just enjoy it and stay calm." A screeching noise brought our conversation to a halt. Mel entered the parking lot at high speed. The rear window of the Fiorino was smashed in.

"Christ, what a mess! What happened? You've wrecked the car, you prick," Luis said, midway between anxiety and smiles. Mel got out of the vehicle, looking pale. Those of us who were sober ran out to the parking lot. "Dude, they almost killed me. I'm alive purely by chance." "What happened?" asked Nairobi. "Where's Vadier?" Then Mel told us what had happened: They had arrived at the village liquor store. The place was full of crazies, beggars, and drunks. Most of them were wearing red shirts, and they were listening to some

turned my stomach. There was even vomit up on the ceiling. The edge of the toilet bowl was covered in the remains of pepper and tomato. Damned Patriot, I said to myself. I remembered that there was a small bathroom on the patio behind the bowls court. I'm profoundly genteel. I need to pee in a toilet bowl. I've never squatted in the bushes in my life. The question of a bathroom is a psychological need, a matter of good breeding. They began to sing a song by Juanes. Nairobi played the guitar. The drunken guys and girls who weren't yet asleep formed a circle around her. I'm bursting, I'm gonna pee in my pants! I walked with short steps. I made it to the small dark room, opened the door, and immediately shut it again. Luis and Titina were inside making out. "Excuse me," I said by reflex. I went back to the kitchen and hid in a sort of laundry room, feeling a bit shaken. At the back of the room, behind a few hanging blankets, was an old washing machine, a seventies model, General Electric, top-loading. When I was a little kid, at my grandmother Leticia's house—Eugenia's mother—there was a machine just like that one, in the room in which I used to shut myself up and play. I opened the lid, lowered down my pants, and sat down. Three minutes later, I felt a huge relief.

My non-reaction was a surprise: I didn't get angry. My experience with Jorge had trained me in the politics of jealousy and meaningless arguments. In our relationship it was natural to get annoyed by anything and everything. Luis, however, was nothing to me. From certain attitudes and comments, I suspected that he liked me, but there was no agreement between us. We hadn't signed a contract of exclusivity. I remembered the day we went to Titina's house. They had greeted each other and said goodbye with huge kisses.

window left me feeling dehydrated. My eyes, elbows, wrists, knees, ankles all hurt. An internal tremor, of a magnitude on the Richter scale, had its epicenter in my left shoulder. Fiery whisky fumes hit my palate. I was getting heat cramps in my sphincter muscle. I was thirsty, very thirsty. I made Luis stop at a gas station to buy some Gatorade. I had dandruff, crusty bits in my eyes, and BO. I'd wanted to take a shower before leaving San Carlos, but the only shower in the house was spattered with vomit. After passing a tollbooth, on a road that turned into a highway, I fell asleep. When I woke up, my hangover, for the most part, had disappeared. Bob Dylan was singing "Stuck Inside of Mobile."

"What've you got going on with Titina?" I asked calmly. He shrugged his shoulders. "Nothing, Titi's my friend." Silence fell between us. Then, after la-la-la-ing the chorus, he added: "I hate the expression 'best friend,' but if I had to describe Titi somehow, that's what it'd be: she's my best friend." He let go of the steering wheel and traced scare quotes in the air. "Why were you arguing?" I asked, staring intently at the landscape. Bit by bit, the horizon was being populated with cows. "We weren't arguing." "Don't shit me, Luis. Yesterday, in the bowls court, you were cursing each other out." He shrugged his shoulders once more. He wanted to say something, and then stopped himself. He gave a heartless smile, and in the end he said: "What I talk about to Titina isn't your problem." He pressed the rewind button. The music resumed with the song "Pledging My Time." Much to my regret, the little whining girl I carry around inside me stirred after his display of hostility. The son of a bitch had managed to hit a nerve. On long stretches of road, all we heard was Dylan. "And what the fuck do we do now?

What's the plan?" I asked not hiding my discontent. "It's late," he said. "I think the best thing would be for us to spend the night in Barinas and then first thing in the morning leave for Altamira de Cáceres." A long silence ensued. "What's wrong? Are you pissed?" he asked impassively. "Visions of Johanna" came on. I heard the harmonica, and I exploded. I pressed the eject button, and tossed the cassette into the back of the car. "What a pain this guy is, Luis! I can't stand him anymore." I opened my backpack, took out my speakers, and turned on my iPod. He grew suddenly pale and silent. His expression, like that of a scolded child, made me laugh. His stupidity provoked my fury. I wanted to upset him, draw blood. I spun the wheel on the iPod, and searched intentionally for something that would end up really disgusting him. At the end of the list I found it: Music> Artist>Paulina Rubio>*Border Girl>*"The One You Love."

I think he had an attack of osteochondritis. He gripped the steering wheel. His mouth improvised a circle of disgust, and his eyes puckered up into small pimples. Light chords, guitar, soft melody. With exaggerated eroticism I lifted up one leg and placed it on top of the dashboard. I leaned back against the door and, resting on my knee, I made a few suggestive movements. I moved my hands like an exotic dancer, chiming in behind Paulina's shrill timbre: "When you're on top of the world / Or it's got you down / When you're flying through the air / Or you're crashing to the ground / When you're searching for the light / And it's nowhere to be found / Just phone me baby . . . (0:32)." I sensed strange noises coming from the back of the car. However, Luis's pained facial expressionw made me ignore the commotion. He put his index finger in his mouth and simulated throwing up.

The Mexican-pop melody made him want to cry. I made out that he was swearing under his breath. A strange drumming sound could be heard coming from the back of the car. Paulina continued: "Baby you can tell me everything / The secrets of your heart / If you could look inside of me / You'd see how beautiful you are... (1:29)." I've always thought I sing badly. However, that time, improvising a pathetic sexy dance, I must say that my voice was at its best—living up to Paulina's standard clearly doesn't take much. The noise from the back of the car returned. Without stopping singing, I turned around to have a look. "I only want to be... I only want to be (1:42)." Utilizing Garay's pliers as a microphone, Vadier suddenly emerged. He raised himself half up and began screeching out the chorus: "Come and get me baby / Let me loose inside your soul / I only want to be your every need / I want to be the girl in all your dreams... (1:55)." An attack of laughter. Luis lost control of the steering wheel. The unexpected laughter made me double over in pain. "Turn it up, turn it up, how fucking cool!" said the apparition in the back of the car. Then, improvising a few classic moves, he sang: "Let me be the lover / You want to uncover... (2:15)." He looked at my face and held up my cheek with his palm. With over-the-top gestures he closed the verse: "Let me be the one you love (2:20)." When the song finished, he explained to us that he had woken up after he felt a bump on the head. He confused the impact of a can of beer with the sharp thump of a Dylan cassette.

ON THE ROAD

1

"We walked in circles for two or three hours," said Vadier. "In the end, the castle looked like a huge mountain." An old man, somewhat lame, served us *cachapas* with butter and cheese. "We stank to high heaven," he continued. "We hadn't taken a shower in six days. We walked single file, with this thing in front"— he gestured with his chin toward Luis —"Floyd in the middle, and me at the end. Have you ever been to Prague?" The expression on my face said no. I was ashamed to admit I hadn't been anywhere, that I was just an armchair Discovery Channel traveler. Vadier the "tri-polar" continued his account in that roadside restaurant: "It's the gloomiest place I've ever been to in my life." I drowned my hangover with a cloying passion fruit juice. The lame guy served us a bowl of fried pork with congealed fat. Luis erupted into fits of raucous laughter. Vadier was strange: skinny, like a bag of bones. I'd never met anyone that thin before. He was wearing a guayabera shirt, Bermuda shorts, and espadrilles. A burlap sack substituted for his backpack. He had terracotta-colored skin and dead-straight hair. He spoke at a leisurely pace, emphasizing his words with gestures of his right hand. He looked like a second-rate Jedi. "We saw a tunnel. This one entered." He gestured toward Luis. "Floyd and I decided to follow him. I read a warning sign in Czech, but paid no attention to it. On it was a tiny black figure with a red line through it. Then, when I searched for the word on the sign in my dictionary, I realized it said 'Danger.' We went all the way in through the dark." He paused for a moment, stretched out his hand, took a sip of his sugarcane juice, and continued. "A tram was headed straight for us. We saw a light in the distance, but we didn't stop. The horn sounded and, at first, we weren't sure what was going on. These guys had gone in about twenty feet. I suddenly realized what was happening. I grabbed my stuff and ducked behind a wall. The tram passed by real close. I thought the guys were done for." Luis smiled quietly, munching on his food. He seemed to recall the event without displeasure. "This guy," Vadier said derisively, "is alive purely by chance. Floyd grabbed him round the neck and shoved him behind a wall. If it weren't for Floyd, this jerk would've been run over and killed by a tram."

2

We were out in the sticks somewhere between Cojedes and Portuguesa. At a suffocating roadside truck stop plastered with Chavista propaganda. The sun was just sadistic. My back was soaked in sweat. I stank, had really bad breath, and my belly button and my knees—behind and in front—itched like crazy. Vadier was talking to himself. Luis laughed halfheartedly. They were recounting shared experiences, anecdotes about trips and failed "happenings." Luis questioned him about his sudden appearance in the Fiorino. Vadier could barely recall accompanying Mel to a liquor store. Then he felt a bump on his head and awoke to a song by Paulina Rubio. It's strange, the most solid friendship I've ever had in my life happened totally by random. They were talking about Floyd. He was such a blob! I remembered the stuff Titina and Nairobi said about him as well: Floyd was an outsider, he didn't belong to the group. Through Vadier's account, I learned that the three of them had backpacked around Europe. My queasiness, brought on by the smell of the butter, distracted me momentarily. Their voices gradually faded into the background. The mountainous horizon threw up questions. The nearness of the specter of my grandfather, Laurent Blanc, aroused childish fears. What would he look like? What would his voice be like? I considered asking Luis to forget about my search, to just drive on and head straight to Mérida to get drunk, to fuck, to do nothing at all, to meet Samuel Lauro, only, please, just not to have to face that figure who provoked both fear and curiosity. The thought of that encounter made my throat clench.

"And where are you two going?" asked the apparition. "Mérida," Luis replied while lighting a cigarette. "And you?" Vadier shrugged his shoulders. "No fucking idea. I was supposed to go to Coro with Mel...Mérida!" he repeated slowly. He traced the name of the town with his finger in the air. Luis asked the lame guy for a pot of coffee. "Querales!" said Vadier. "That rat Querales is in Mérida," he added. "Dude, would it be OK if I tagged along on this trip, if you drove me to Mérida? I'd like to drop in on that punk at his place." For a moment, silence fell between us. Luis looked at me with an air of doubt. "What do you say, *Eugénie*?" he asked in a mock French accent. Fucking great, I said to myself. The thought of extra company bothered me to some degree. The prospect of being alone with Luis was much more appealing. But then, in his moments of lucidity, Vadier could be quite funny. Vadier kept staring at us with the expression of a losing contestant on *American Idol.* He was anxiously awaiting a favorable verdict. "We'll be in Mérida tomorrow or the day after, it all depends," said Luis. "I'm knackered. We'll stay in Barinas tonight. Tomorrow we're going to Altamira de Cáceres, a remote town in the paramo, and we'll decide if we stay there the night or if we continue on. Is that OK with you?" He shrugged again. "Don't worry about me, I can sleep in the Fiorino. I won't bother you. My presence," he said, raising his right hand and swearing an oath, "won't disturb your intimacy." A long silence ensued after that. "So that rat Querales is in Mérida!" Luis said, breaking the icy tension. "Yeah," Vadier replied, "he had to split because of some trouble his old man got into. You know that Old Man Querales worked at PDVSA, the state oil company. That asshole got involved with the opposition, who called for the general strike, and got himself pretty fucked up when that didn't work out, lost all his money. Old Lady Querales cheated on him, and the dumbass, Rafa, had to come up to Mérida with his sister and the cuckold." "It's been ages since I saw that son of a bitch." "Me too. I think the last time I saw him was when Mel screwed María Lionza." "Holy shit!" Small chuckle. "OK," I said, adjusting myself in my seat to

and began spouting all kinds of obscenities. Mel perched atop the goddess, leaned back against her, and plastered her with sloppy kisses. 'Mari, I love you. Mari, I want to make love to you,' he said to her. And so, with those rats forming a threesome with the goddess of Sorte Mountain, dawn broke." Bob Dylan began to sing "I Want You."

4

And, once again, "Visions of Johanna." I protested. Vadier had fallen asleep. "Christ, Luis, how annoying! Let's listen to something else. I can't stand this guy any longer." "Princess, please." "Don't call me Princess, you know it makes me mad." I looked for my iPod. Indifferent to his tantrum, I placed the speakers on the dashboard. "Let's make a deal, Luis. From now on, for every one of Dylan's songs, we'll hear one of mine, agreed? What's more, every time you put on 'Visions of Johanna,' I'll put on my favorite song." "And what's your favorite song?" he asked calmly, convinced that I wouldn't have a reply. What do I know! I said to myself: whatever song, whatever ballad. I didn't know what to say. In truth, I had a varied taste in music, without any particular preferences. "'Peter Pan' by El Canto del Loco," I said, just to say something, because I'd read the title a few seconds before that, in the list on the iPod. "El Canto del Loco!" he repeated sarcastically. "Christ, Eugenia, how can you take some guy who calls himself El Canto del Loco seriously?" "It's not a guy, it's a group." "Even worse. They must be real crap because of that name." "They're cool. Their lyrics are great." "'Their lyrics are great!'" he mocked me. I wanted to hit him. "Yeah," he added smugly, "I imagine they're grand poets. El Canto del Loco might become the Beat Generation of the twenty-first century. They're probably the Dadaists of the new millennium." "Shut up already. I can't stand you." Despite his offensive mood, he won me over with his cultured persona. "'Visions of Johanna' has great lyrics. Do you know what it's about?" I didn't respond. I let my gaze wander to the glove compartment, to the image of Our Lady Rosa Mystica. "It's the story of Louise," he added. "Do you know what 'Johanna' stands for?" I looked at him without interest. "Go on, Luis, enlighten me, explain it all." He ignored my sarcasm. "*Gehenna* is the Hebrew name for Hell. Louise is this cool, regular girl, who goes through some things in her life. She observes the world around her and often has visions of Hell. Listen carefully." Then he translated a few lines: "*He brags of his misery, he likes to live dangerously.*" He let the song play and then added, "*And these visions of Johanna are now all that remain.* It's poetry, Princess... It's totally awesome. Have you read Kerouac?" "No, Luis, I haven't read Kerouac, nor do I know who the hell Kerouac is." "They say the title of Dylan's song was inspired by Kerouac, by his novel *Visions of Cody* or *Visions of Gerard*. Dylan is a phenomenon. In his lyrics you'll discover Shakespeare, Eliot. But of course, your Locos are probably equally brilliant." "Screw you!" I said with a grin. Unexpectedly, he pressed the eject button and invited me to turn on the iPod. "Let's do something, Eugenia. Let's listen to your Locos. I want you to put on that shit, 'Peter Pan,' and explain its poetry to me." "Don't shit me, Luis." "I'm serious. Put on the Locos. I want to hear what you've got to say, what they say, what they do. In twenty years, no one'll remember those guys. On the other hand, Dylan's immortal."

Minutes later: Music>Artist>El Canto del Loco>*Personas* (10 songs)>"Peter Pan." 6 of 10. Acoustic guitar, calm, blue, low. It may not have been my favorite song, but I definitely liked it a lot: "One day, calmness comes over me / My Peter Pan rouses today / There's little left to do here (0:20)." Luis laughed in a low voice. "I feel like I'm somewhere else / Somewhere alone at home / It'll be your skin that's to blame (0:30)." Luis: "God!" "It must be because I've grown older / That something new has pressed this button / For Peter to leave (0:40)." Luis: "Dear Mother of God!" "And maybe now I'll live much better / More at ease and at peace inside myself. / May Tinkerbell take care of you and watch over you (0:52)." He opened his mouth, forming a perfect circle. He covered the hole with his palm and said in a very low voice, "What horror." "At times you shout from the heavens / Wanting to destroy all my calm / Coming after me like thunder / To give me that bolt of blue lightning. / Now you shout to me from the heavens / But you encounter my soul / Don't try anything with me / It seems that love calms me down… it calms me down (1:17)." "Enough already, please," he said. "I can't stand anymore. Turn that shit off."

"Damn, how cool, El Canto del Loco," Vadier called out in a sleepy voice. Nevertheless, the mass of flesh hunched up in the back of the car remained impassive. "OK, Princess, let's hear it then, give me your poetry reading. Explain the meaning of the song." "Shut up." "Princess, I'm serious, tell me what you think." What do I think? I said to myself. I don't know, I don't think, I don't know how to think. "Shut your mouth, Luis Tévez." I didn't know what to say. He kept pressing me and asking me until it nearly drove me round the bend. I felt the song could be talking about anything:

"The song's talking about the passage of time. It's talking about what it means to grow up. It says that growing up is a piece of shit." "Philosophy pure and simple," he said with a sardonic expression on his face. "Drop dead. It's somewhat conventional, Luis, a bit too mundane for you"— I'd never used the word "mundane" before —"and that's precisely the poetry in it. It's a song for normal people, not for intense ones like you. You can listen to Dylan the amazing, the profound, the mystical, the whatever, but to me, that dumbass says nothing at all. Those guys talk about the passage of time, about the horror and the awe of what it means to be a kid, to want to be older and, at the same time, not to want it. A problem that a gifted guy like you would never understand." A round of applause interrupted my speech. Vadier peered out from the back of the car and asked me if I had anything by Juanes. Luis slammed on the brakes suddenly. Traffic. Heaps of traffic. The bends in the Portuguesa Highway, banked up with cars, looked like an anthill.

5

"*¡Qué güevo!*—what a pain!" said Luis on seeing the traffic jam. He tried turning on the air-conditioner, and a noise came from under the hood. A smell of meatballs, accompanied by a puff of smoke, invaded the Fiorino. "*Güevo, güevo!*" Vadier repeated. "It's strange," he said. "In Venezuela the word *güevo* is a misleading term." His face had lost its freshness from just a while back. He seemed absent, withdrawn, lost in an alternate reality. His eyes were crusty with sleep, a thick string of snot dangled from his nose. The disgust I felt caused me to focus my attention on the signs advertising goats for sale. "Despite the fact they're

a radio. "It's strange, Luis, don't you think? It doesn't make sense: superlatives are meant to modify nouns to signify the highest attainable level or degree of something. If to be a *güevo* implies being 'badass,' then to be a *güevón* should imply that you're 'the biggest badass'; but no, to be a *güevón* is the same as being 'a dumbass,' the exact opposite. And then, on the other hand, there's the participle: *la güevonada.* This is even more curious." Luis laughed to himself. He covered his mouth and seemed to be muttering curses under his breath. "Let's suppose that this traffic jam is due to an accident. We move forward, we pass the bend, and we see a car wedged under a truck. We see blood, arms, heads, and other parts. The natural thing to say would be: *¡Una güevonada!* This participle implies astonishment, surprise, shock. It's somewhat hardcore. But on the other hand, the same participle can imply triviality, superficiality, irrelevance. If, for example, Eugenia says that such and such is important, Luis could simply disagree and say that it's just a *güevonada.* And here, once again, a strange linguistic contrast is made, wouldn't you agree?" The traffic started to move. The distracted drivers returned to their cars. A Zephyr overheated and had to pull over. "There are more misunderstandings with respect to the word *güevo.*" I couldn't stop myself from laughing. Vadier's lecture was so funny, his expression solemn, and besides, the way he explained things was enjoyable. "If we say that so-and-so is a *cabeza'e güevo,* then we're saying he's an idiot or a 'dickhead.' Strictly speaking, the word *güevo* refers literally to the glans. The glans in this case being synonymous with 'dickhead.' Thus, if so-and-so is a *cabeza'e güevo,* then his stupidity is not in doubt. But, on the other hand, let's say so-and-so is a *güevo pela'o—*

which refers literally to an erect penis with the foreskin pulled back—then in this case we're saying he's intelligent or a 'clever dick.' But I ask you: What difference is there between a *güevo pela'o* and the head of a *güevo*? Wouldn't a *güevo pela'o* be an exposed glans? Aren't we talking about the same thing here? Why then—"

"Enough already! Christ, stop wanking on so much," shouted Luis. "They're just some of my musings, Luis, don't get angry. What do you think, Eugenia?" "I think you're a philosopher," I said to him, laughing to myself while opening up a bag of Doritos that I found in my bag. "I'd never thought about it that way before. You're right." "Language is very deceptive," he added. The traffic advanced. On passing the bend, we saw the checkpoint. Ten municipal police, disguised in military gear, were standing guard in front of a shanty with a line of orange cones across the highway. Luis swore loudly. Old tires served as a makeshift barrier. Two gorillas approached the Fiorino. "Stop on the right-hand side, citizen," said the lesser of the simians. After asking us a few trivial questions, they told us to get out of the vehicle.

BARINAS

1

The officer's eyes were like two fried eggs. He had a pimple-like bump on the edge of one of his eyelids. "Hide it, hide it," said the second gorilla, nervously handing Luis a plastic bag to disguise the bottle. "OK, citizen, on your way now," ordered the cop after the friendly deal was completed. The raid on Uncle Germán's barracks spared us a stint in jail.

Vadier had lost his ID card; besides which, his clothes stank of pot. The cops asked to see ludicrous documents: certified certificates, authorized authorizations, signed by sham ministries. Vadier explained that his ID card had been stolen at a liquor store in San Carlos, but the impassive policemen just threatened to arrest him. Luis was struck dumb, rendered speechless. The gray-faced simian suggested that our "trivial" dispute could be resolved by doing a deal. I didn't give it a second thought. I walked over to the car, opened the back door, and reached inside. The gorillas got nervous. One of them even pulled a gun on me. The sun's rays hitting the bottle blinded them. The sight of

Blue Label—like an apparition of the Blessed Virgin Mary herself—took them by surprise. Minutes later, they stowed away their payoff in the patrol car, told us the best route to take, and, with their blessing, let us go.

2

Barinas, like all the other suffocating small towns in Venezuela, was horrible. The town was plastered with out-of-date electoral propaganda. A poster with the slogan "Forward" and the photo of a fat guy named Oswaldo Álvarez Paz hung from a broken-down traffic light. The sandy streets were full of garbage. Water bubbled up through the storm drains like fountains, but with groups of beggars, in place of naked goddesses, spitting out the filthy liquid. A gas-station attendant recommended a motel to us just outside of town, in Barinitas. The roads had suffered badly from torrential downpours in the past. There were potholes everywhere. Chavez posters lined the cracked walls and the roller doors. "Damned Revolution" read some orange-colored graffiti at the entrance to an abandoned hospital. Without any warning, the main street became a dirt road. Packs of mangy dogs roamed the bends in search of scraps of food. The street kids, admonished by their mothers, refused to share their findings with the starved animals. I've seen some ugly places in the world, but rarely have I seen any place more disgusting than Barinas.

We took a cheap room with cable TV, a VHS player, and hot water. Vadier asked to borrow my iPod. He stayed in the Fiorino, cheerfully listening to the latest album by Melendi. It was a small pentagon-shaped room. Luis threw himself on the bed. He turned on the television, landing on a channel with some interracial porn in extreme close up. "Cool!" he said. The bathroom was a mushroom colony. Besides that, it had no door. The shower stall was rusty, the floor tiles were cracked, and the plastic shower curtain, which at one time had been transparent, had stiff curly hairs stuck to it. Coagulated soap scum clogged the drain hole. My bowels sang praises at the sight of the toilet bowl—without a lid, with traces of rust, but a toilet bowl all the same. My belly was swollen, hot. For the past few hours, a burning sensation had been putting my sphincter muscles to the test. The need to "go" made that filthy receptacle seem to me like a luxurious commode. "Luis, can you get outta here," I shouted. "What's up, Princess?" he said, without taking his eyes off the TV. Out of the corner of my eye I could see three black women reaching orgasm on top of a pool table. "I want you to go out for a bit." He gave no reaction, so I added: "I don't know... go out and buy some bread or something with Vadier. I need to take a shower, and I want to have a shit. If you're here, I can't do it. So beat it." "Don't worry, don't take any notice of me," he said, settling down on the creaky mattress. I fixed him with an angry stare that made him back down. "OK, Princess. I'll go out for a short walk. I'll be back in thirty minutes." "Forty-five." "OK, I'll be back in forty-five." When he shut the door behind him, I raced to the bathroom. I've never understood how the body is capable of generating so much waste. I've always thought that if God is responsible for the shit, then all that stuff about image and likeness raises certain questions for which no one has offered any convincing answers.

3

"Samuel Lauro set up the Poetic Sabotage forum," Vadier explained. "It was a meeting place for misfits and renegades. Luis was in Belgium. Mel—the wandering 'screw'—was taking a year off, traveling through the slums of Rome. In some way, Samuel enabled us to keep in touch. It was a find, a pretext, a way of doing things. Later on, as always, it all went to shit." We were in a grocery store that the proprietor of the motel—Señora Maigualida (a mass of human flesh weighing four hundred pounds)—had told us about.

"Take a shower!" I had ordered Luis when he got back to the room. He just screwed up his face. "You smell like shit. You stink like a sewer," I said to him. He threw a huge tantrum, saying that he didn't usually take a shower when he was on vacation. I grabbed a bar of soap and put it in his hands. "If you don't take a shower, you can sleep in the Fiorino with Vadier." He took his time replying. He grabbed his JanSport backpack and, after passing through the door-frame without a door, began to undress. I hesitated: my curiosity to see him naked came up against fierce resistance from my sense of decency, Catholic guilt, and his bad smell. He took off his T-shirt and threw it to the ground. He had a pale, star-shaped scar across his shoulder. I recalled the schoolyard rumor in Natalia's strident voice: at one time Luis had been shot.

The memory of Natalia was a reminder of unavoidable obligations. I left the room and called Caracas. "Hi, Mom, everything's fine. Yeah, everything's great, bye. Amen," I replied to her icy blessing. I had four messages from Natalia: three texts and one voicemail. Her melodramatic carrying-on led me to believe a farce was underway. I spoke to her a few minutes later: Gonzalo had cut his forehead. He had to have twelve stitches. Drunk, trying to get the attention of some college girls by the pool, he had miscalculated his dive. He mistook the deep end for the shallow and hit his head. The pool filled up with blood. "Bitch, it was horrible," said Natalia. "It happened around three in the morning. They took him to a clinic in Chichiriviche until daybreak and then transferred him to the hospital, where they stitched him up. The doctors recommended rest, but my folks want to leave for Caracas today. You should've been here," she said in a moralistic tone. "Are you fucking kidding me, Natalia?" I hung up. I walked around the motel parking lot in circles. Fake moaning from the porno could be heard through the wooden doors. I came across Vadier chatting to some fat woman. He smiled. He seemed normal. He didn't give the impression that he was going to turn into a werewolf or start expounding linguistic theories on human feces. Light and darkness competed against each other in the sky. "Eugenia, let's go buy some food!" he said. "I'll make a salad for you and Luis." Amid a burst of laughter, the fat woman gave us the directions to the grocery store.

"The problem with Luis is that he thinks he's a badass," Vadier said as we walked down a path between two old sidewalks. "Don't believe anything he says. He just rehashes all those stupid things he gets from Bob Dylan, the Rolling Stones, and Janis Joplin. If Paulina Rubio was called Pauline Blondie, that dumbass would say that she was cool. The dude's been like that since he was a little kid. The same as his old man, Armando: a bullshit artist and stuck-up. Once, in seventh grade, Mel fucked him over like no one else before.

Whenever someone brings it up, the dude gets real mad. Mel, the rat, told him that he had tickets to the Bob Marley concert. 'Yeah, really, that's awesome!' Luis replied. 'I'm gonna go with my old man.'" The story ended abruptly. The expression on Vadier's face suggested that the outcome was funny. I shrugged my shoulders without getting the joke.

We arrived at the grocery store. The place was named after a saint. A stereotypical Portuguese Creole man stood guard at the entrance. The smell inside the place was hard to define: household cleaner mixed with tuna and mortadella. That dump gave credence to the cliché of the typical musty store. Vadier grabbed a shopping basket and began filling it with strange salad greens. Parsley, celery, spinach? I wondered. No idea. He picked up the tomatoes, fingered them, sniffed them, and, undecided, put them back in their smelly wooden crates. He asked for a pound of potatoes and two onions. "I'll make a Caesar, Caprese, and a Roman salad. How does that sound?" he asked. "I don't eat a lot of greens, but whatever." "Hey, Maestro! Do you have any chicken?" The Creole man placed a disgusting carcass on the wooden bench. "Titina and Luis?" Vadier said, puzzled. I took advantage of his good mood to ask him a few questions. "Not that I know of. They're just friends. Titina and Luis have known each other since they were kids." "Do you know why they fought?" I asked. "They had a fight? I didn't know they had a fight. Don't take any notice of them. Those dudes get into it every other week." "I don't know, Vadier," I said. "I think I fucked up. Maybe she thinks I'm going out with Luis, that I'm banging her guy." The Creole man offered us some sausage and chorizo. Vadier asked for a quarter pound of each. "I don't think so, Eugenia. Titina wouldn't get pissed about that. Hey, Maestro! You wouldn't happen to have any red wine hidden away around here?" The Creole man rummaged in a freezer that looked like an old-fashioned icebox from the 1930s and came across something awful called "Piccolino." Vadier asked for two plastic cups. That wine tasted like tamarind-flavored Tang. The kindly Creole man invited us to sit down at a small table. Darkness blanketed the sky. After swallowing another gulp of wine, Vadier told me that Titina had probably gotten angry with Luis because of his determination to meet up with Samuel Lauro.

"Samuel Lauro set up the Poetic Sabotage forum," he said. I knew that Samuel Lauro had created a website, blog, or social networking site frequented mainly by Venezuelans in exile. "It was a hoot," he said. "Visiting that page was really great, because you would come across all kinds of craziness. At first, no one believed any of it would be taken seriously." "And what did they do?" "Stupid things!" he replied. "There were various proposals in the 'About Us' section. For example, some guy who lives in Barcelona suggested blowing up this shithole. He had a really cool PDF map that showed the Caribbean Sea extending across Brazil and Colombia. Venezuela was completely submerged. People wrote comments and debated stuff in the forum. It was all just a joke." Third swallow of Piccolino. "There were the neorealists as well: some guys who proposed reverting to the old colonial status of Captaincy General of Venezuela and reintegrating with the Kingdom of Spain. They collected signatures, wrote hymns, published manifestos. But, without a doubt, the coolest thing about the forum was the terrorism. Samuel started a discussion thread called 'Poetic

Terrorism.' It was all about coming up with ideas for small acts of sabotage that would fuck up Chavismo. Do you know who William Lara is?" "Not a fucking clue," I replied. The Creole man began turning off the lights in the grocery store. "A Chavista minister, deputy, or some shit like that. One day, that dumbass was having lunch at some grill downtown. Someone spotted him and sent a tip-off to the forum. The most warrior-like of the poetic terrorists was Pelolindo. I'm not sure if Luis had come back from Belgium at that time. I don't think he had. Pelolindo went to the restaurant with Mel. They hid in the parking lot for a while, and when they spotted the dude asking for the check, they sprayed some Liquid Ass in his car. The deputy had to take a cab. They took photos and put them up on the web page. It was all a joke. Stupid things like that, Eugenia, pure clowning around. Screwing over Chavistas. One day, they punctured the tires and stole the hood off Aristóbulo's car; another time, during a United Socialist Party march, they threw tar in Iris Varela's hair. With over one hundred twenty members, the forum filled with all sorts of crazy ideas. That's where they hatched up the plan of scratching Fernando Carrillo's car and spitting on Nicolás Maduro's pizza. Between one idea and another, things began to degenerate. Things were getting heavier. Samuel was the website administrator. He portrayed himself as a cool dude. He sold himself as a poet-liberator, because the other thing that that rat did was write protest poetry, verses as performance pieces. Some were good. I remember one called 'Fort Tiuna Military Base, or Facility of Shit.' People sent their dumbass ideas to the website, and others commented on them. As I said before, at first everything was really cool.

accused of incitement to crime, illegal assembly, and who knows what other shit. Those guys are screwed now."

The country road was inhabited by specters. We were shadowed on our brief walk by numerous thugs. Dammit to hell if they don't rape or kill me in this shit of a town! My walking companion was calm. His perpetual smile, amid the anxiety, gave me a strange sense of security. Vadier spoke about Prague, about high school, about Daniel. He told me that he had definitely made a fool of himself at the Suárez house, where my brother and his classmates had celebrated their graduation. Weeks after his impertinent question, he called Señora Lidia to ask her forgiveness. "By the way, do you have a joint?" he asked me after passing by a squalid corner. I told him I didn't. "I have to get one for tonight. One of these thugs must have a stash. If not, I'll ask Señora Maigualida," he said. "Who's Señora Maigualida?" "The proprietor of the motel, the fat woman." "How did you meet her?" "I don't know. She was watching TV. I passed by, and we started chatting. I like people. I'm not antisocial like Luis." "I wouldn't say that Luis hates people; I think it's just that he's afraid of people." "Yeah, that's true. He's people-phobic." "So then, you guys went backpacking around Europe?" I asked. On the walk back, the motel seemed much farther away. The neon lights advertising a hot tub and VHS could be seen in the distance. "No," said Vadier. "Luis went with Floyd. I met them over there. I was in Paris. When I found out that they were going to Vienna and Prague, I caught a train and met up with them." I remembered the stories about Floyd. "He's a real blob!" I said aloud. "Where did Floyd come from?" Vadier let out a sputtering laugh that turned into a cough. "The story about

Floyd is a real crack-up. You won't believe it." "Tell me." We were crossing through a stretch of scrub. Vadier seemed to be mulling over his words and his story. "Do you like soap operas?" he asked. "No," I replied, "not much." "Everything about Floyd is a Mexican soap opera. It's a sensational storyline." "A what?" "Nothing, it's something completely bizarre." "C'mon! Tell me already!" We arrived at the gate. Vadier placed his hands on my shoulders: "Luis and Floyd are brothers.

"In eighth grade, our English teacher gave us an assignment to create a video. It was Titi, Luis, and me. We decided to make a kind of news report. My camera was fucked. When I took it out of my bag, I realized that the lens was broken. Luis's was a piece of nineties crap. It didn't have a USB port, which would make editing the video a real problem. Luis told us that his old man had a video camera at the factory. He called up Armando, asked if he could borrow it, and we went to pick it up. I remember it all clearly. We caught a cab. We arrived at Los Ruices, and that clown, Garay, handed us a briefcase. 'Luisito, this is for you, from your father.'" Vadier imitated the watchman's voice perfectly. "It was hardcore. I took a look at the video camera and realized there was a disk inside. There was a name written on the disk in permanent marker: Marco. What's this shit? I said to myself. When I pressed "Play" and put my eye to the viewfinder, I saw Old Man Armando changing some little kid's diaper. I fast-forwarded a bit and saw him making out with some chick with milk-white skin, an albino. Then he kissed and cuddled the newborn. Another albino, a lot bigger, was playing with him. It was the first time I saw Floyd." We entered the motel. I went with Vadier to the reception. Señora Maigualida was watching *Jesus of Nazareth*. She greeted us warmly, as if we'd been neighbors for years, inviting us in and offering us some cheese sticks. Vadier asked her a favor. He explained that he wanted to make some salads and that he'd need to heat some water and borrow a few utensils. The fat lady was terrific. She said that her gas cooker and her saucepans were at our disposal. Six or seven little kids ran down the corridor. "Old Man Armando was leading a double life. He'd been going out with that albino chick for ages and had two kids with her. Floyd, whose name probably isn't really Floyd at all, was the first. I think Floyd's real name is José or Juan or Ramón or Pablo. I'm not really sure." "And why do they call him Floyd?" "How should I know? For some crazy reason." Vadier began to wash the lettuce. He asked me politely to cut up some small pieces of bread. Señora Maigualida gave us some warm beer. "Floyd's a weirdo," I said. "He's a really strange guy." "Yeah, it's true, he's a little touched in the head. They put him in a special school. The dude's a little crazy, but he's cool. He's loyal to Luis." "And what happened? How did they meet?" "Luis found out from that video that he had two brothers." Vadier chopped up the lettuce into small pieces and then sprinkled some parmesan over the leaves. "He spoke to his old man and asked him what all that shit was about. Armando had no choice but to intro-duce them. I don't know how it happened, but all of a sudden, Luis began hanging out with his brother, and they became friends. They did a photography course together, and gradually, Floyd became a part of our group. I think Señora Aurora knew all about that mess, but she played dumb. After that, they went to Europe, and, well, Floyd had

previously shown a profound contempt. The existential angst I was so fond of displaying fell apart in a motel. I had never been seduced by words before.

Vadier prepared various salads. We toasted each other with water, because we were hungover. We discussed some popular gringo TV shows, shared some anecdotes, and if I remember correctly, we speculated on the origin of earthquakes. The Caprese salad tasted good. As I've already hinted, my diet didn't consist of healthy food, much less the consumption of salads and vegetables. The chicken Caesar salad, a dish I'd refused to eat throughout my adolescent years, also pleased my fussy palate. Aside from satisfying my hunger, the food was really good.

Luis had taken a shower and shaved. Just before dinner, I asked for some privacy to use the bathroom without a door. On top of the toilet, I saw a black bag with lotions and expensive aftershave. The sight of that kit made me feel ashamed of my cheap deodorant. I developed a complex about my unmistakable smell of hotel soap. That night Luis had on a white T-shirt with the faded image of an old politician whose name, he told me, was Jaime Lusinchi. The word YES in block letters was printed on the back. He wore yellow board shorts and a pair of Timberland sandals. His strong and hairy legs invited odious comparisons with Jorge's skinny ones. I was wearing a plain pastel-blue dress. After the salads, he sat down on the bed and lit a cigarette. Taking the piss out of my royal nickname, Vadier told me to remain seated. Bowing down and calling me "Your Highness," he said that he would take care of the dishes. Luis was smoking and staring intently into my eyes. His calm expression was intimidating. I don't like being stared at. I can't stand it. Luis made me feel like a quadriplegic at a salsa school. Vadier was talking to himself. He was recounting sensational stories about Querales, Mel, and the eternal misfits. Summoning up strength, I decided to confront Luis. I raised my head and looked at him. "OK, OK, I get it," Vadier said. "I know when I'm not wanted. I'm leaving. Relax. Take it easy. I'll be in the Fiorino, if you need me." The well-mannered cook went out and shut the door behind him.

Ultimately, Jorge had made the first move. After a day of suggestive glances on the beach, he approached me and kissed me on the mouth. Then—hurting me without meaning to—he awkwardly thrust his trembling hand down my pants. Although he'd been the one to take the initiative, gradually, over time, I became the chief conductor. For his part, Luis just smoked and stared at me. He didn't say a word, he didn't move, he didn't come close. His statue-like expression completely immobilized me. Amid the smoke and the silence, desire threatened to develop into an aneurysm. Time passed miserably slowly. When he finished his cigarette, Luis threw the butt in a can of Coke and lay down on the bed with his hands behind his neck. "It's late, Princess. We should go to sleep." I got up from the table and drank a glass of water. He lay face down on the bed and covered his head with the pillow. I cursed his calmness, his delaying tactics. All my neurotic, girlish fears burst through to the surface: Doesn't he like me? Does he think I'm ugly? Is he in love with Titina? My sense of confusion compelled me to confront him. I grabbed an old beat-up chair, flipped it around, and straddled it, leaning my arms on the backrest. "Luis." He seemed to wake up. "What happened?" he said groggily. "Do you like me?" He just blinked in incomprehension. He yawned and sat up. "What's up with you?" he said halfheartedly. "Nothing. I want to know if you like me. Your attitude confuses me." "What attitude?" he asked, sitting up. "You...I don't know what you want from me. I don't know what we're doing in this dump." "We've come here to find your French grandfather. You want to leave this shitty country, don't you? Better to be in a motel room than out in some parking lot, don't you think?" He crossed his legs on the bed and, after banging the pack of cigarettes on the night table, took out a Marlboro Red. From being the one asking all the questions, I had unexpectedly ended up being interrogated. I didn't know how to respond. I didn't know what the right answer should be. The worst thing is that he seemed to be in control of the situation. He seemed to anticipate my reactions. I grew angry. I felt bold and brazen. I became quite rude at his continued dismissals. "Are you gay?" "I beg your pardon?" "Are you a fag?" I said. He just laughed. "How narrow-minded you are, Eugenia. You're just like all those other Caracas snobs. You think that if you're alone with a man and he doesn't want to be with you, that obviously means he's gay. You have a blinkered view of human relationships." Bastard! I felt small and weak. I felt defeated. That claustrophobic room reminded me of the high school volleyball court. The only other person who had made me feel so humiliated was my PE teacher. He continued smoking. "What is it you want, Eugenia? To fuck? OK, that's cool with me. Let's fuck." He pulled back the blanket and patted the mattress beside him. "Well, c'mon then. You can start off with a blow job." "Christ, you really are vulgar!" "Don't get angry, Princess. You're the one who wants me," the son of a bitch said to me.

my knees. "It's strange, Princess. With you, I'd like to go walking through the mall or make out at a movie. I'd like to take you to see the otters in the lake at East Park or have a banana split at an ice cream parlor. With you, more than just fucking, I'd like to make love." He went out of the room. "I'll be back," he said. His confession left me dazed. I spent the next few minutes staring blankly, going over what he had said, trying to grasp unforeseen events and ominous silences. He returned with a bottle of Blue Label. He poured two shots and offered me the smallest of the two. "Let's make a deal, Princess. We've got at least two more nights together. Maybe three, it depends. I promise that, on our last night together, we'll make love. For now, the best thing is to enjoy the sexual tension. Cheers!" He clinked his glass against mine. "Sexual tension?" I hadn't lost the moronic habit of echoing his words. "Yeah, sexual tension, horniness, desire, knowing that something could happen, and feeling the frustration because nothing does. Knowing that while I was undressing in the bathroom you were watching me from the door. The heat in your fingers when you light my cigarettes. The desire to touch you, and not touching you. Knowing you're there, and not there. The certainty of pleasure, and the dread of doubt. That kind of tension is really cool, don't you think?" "You're crazy, Luis Tévez. You're a really strange guy," I said lamely, just to say something. I didn't know how to act. I didn't know whether to look at him, touch him, or give him a friendly hug. The atmosphere favored an erotic distance. "I'm a damned capitalist, Princess. My problem is that I believe in private property." Huh? I said to myself, what's he talking about? "Believe me, if we fuck today, or if we'd fucked yesterday, everything would have gone to shit. I'm a fucked-up zelophobe. I know it. Possession turns me into a beast. I've done a lot of stupid things. I've sacrificed many friendships just for a fuck, for a bad, fleeting fuck. I don't want to screw things up with you. If we make sure our last night together is special"— he made scare quotes with his fingers around the last word —"we might have time to think things through, to sort it all out. We wouldn't have the pressure of being together all the time, like on this trip. We could see each other at school, but I would understand that your mind is elsewhere, that you have other interests, that you have a boyfriend. I wouldn't have to wake up tomorrow morning, look you in the face, and realize that all of this has been total bullshit." "My relationship with Jorge is bullshit, Luis. If I have to break up with him, I'll do it. I don't care." "Break up for what reason? To get involved with me? Why would you do that? So that, in two weeks or four months or, if everything goes well for us, in a year, you get sick of me? So that, one day, you can tell some other guy that your relationship is bullshit? Jorge might be a dumbass, but perhaps he's a noble one." He poured himself another shot of whisky and took a slow sip. He put his glass on the table and sat down in front of me. He ran his fingers through my hair. I felt a shiver. "I don't want to fuck things up with you, Princess." However, the tender moment was soon displaced by his inevitable vulgarity. "So it was that asshole, Jorge, who popped your cherry?" "Christ, Luis, you're a real... jerk." "Well, OK then, I'll put it another way," he added. He took another gulp of his drink. "Did you lose your virginity to Jorge?" "Yes, Luis, I did." "Cool," he replied. "How long ago?" "I don't know, last year. About this time last year."

"Coming outside is a rip off. It's like drinking non-alcoholic beer or decaffeinated coffee. Of course, it all depends on which part of the body you come on." "It's disgusting." "What is?" he asked. "That shit. Semen. It's warm, it looks like lumpy soup, it stinks, and its texture is extremely unpleasant. If that puddle of shit is the origin of life, then I know why humanity is a scrap heap." "I like your philosophical rants." He came up and kissed me on the mouth. A light kiss, without saliva, without tongue, barely brushing his face against mine. He touched his lips against mine and withdrew. "Do you have your iPod?" he asked. "You told me that, among all that crap, you have a few good songs." "Let me see if it's here." I lay down on the bed and looked in my backpack. I gave him the device while I tried to find the speakers amid the jumble of clothes and other useless bits and pieces. "What a load of junk this iPod is," he said while reviewing the playlist. He reached over with his left hand and played with my hair. "You have some really cool songs, but most of them are crap. Fuck! How cool!" he shouted. "Put this one on." I turned on the speakers and connected the device. "Come here, Princess, let's dance." Music>Artist>R.E.M.>"Losing My Religion." He took me by the waist and invited me out onto the patch of cement. After pretending to strum a guitar, he sang the lyrics in my ear in very phony English. In general, I loathe embraces and lovey-doveyness, but during that gentle waltz, I managed to forget all my qualms about body contact. "What will you say to your grandfather tomorrow, Princess? Do you think we'll find him?" he asked me during the chorus. "I don't know. I'm scared, Luis. I feel like just going straight on and forgetting the name of that town forever. What I want to do is stupid. Finding him or not won't change anything. Something tells me I'll never leave Caracas." "What the hell," he said, "we'll see what happens. We're almost there." The song ended, and we continued hugging for about five minutes. Remembering that scene brings with it the sounds of fireflies, crickets, grasshoppers, and other useless animals, now but a sweet memory. "Go to bed, Princess. It's late." He kissed me on the forehead and went out to smoke a cigarette. I used his chest as a pillow. His right hand rested on my shoulder. He told me that, in order to trick insomnia, he liked to count butchered sheep. We took turns counting to two hundred and twenty-four.

ALTAMIRA DE CÁCERES

1

"Laurent Blanc disappeared," a mysterious messenger would inform me. "The old man told the world to take a hike and then went off to meet the devil." I woke up with a stiff neck. Luis didn't speak to me all morning. The romance was gone. The cold light of day undid our pact. The feeble lovey-dovey things that people in love usually say to each other when they wake up weren't given a chance to be uttered. He took a long, loud piss and didn't flush. He left the room without a word. Then he spent over an hour sitting on the hood of the Fiorino, smoking the whole time.

My nose was stuffy, and I had a headache. I stumbled out of bed, zigzagging to the bathroom. I banged into the table. A glass with the dregs of cloudy whisky crashed to the floor and shattered. My early morning clumsiness caused me to step on a shard of glass, which resulted in excessive bleeding. I wiped my foot with the pillowcase. I had the strange feeling that it would turn out to be a terrible day. What I never imagined was that an unexpected

Landa." That name prompted one of the few laughs of the day. "Yeah, that's him, a skinny old guy with the face of a sadist." "Jeez, Eugenia, Landa's a real institution! Most of those horrible films that we burned the other day excluded Landa. He's the only 'good' one out there," he said, resuming his mocking tone. "Anyway, what I wanted to tell you is: for a number of years, my father was a member of the crew on that show. He liked to call himself an actor. But really, he was just a lighting assistant or stagehand or he carried the cables or took photocopies or who the fuck knows what. Alfonso was just another one of the jerks at Venevisión. He appeared on it once or twice." "How cool!" Luis said. "Cool my ass. Do you remember what the show was like? Some of the sketches would take place in a café or a restaurant, in which case extras were required; some losers had to sit around the other tables to give the impression that the place was full. That's where Alfonso came in. Those were my dad's only appearances on TV. Later, when the show folded, Alfonso dedicated himself to the honorable task of being an extra." When I said the word "honorable," I raised my hands and made scare quotes in the air with my fingers, copying one of Luis's gestures. It was the first time I'd ever done that in my life. "It was an awful show. And the worst part is, the bastard would tape it and force us to watch it on weekends. He's an asshole, Luis. The creep would be ad-libbing in the background, overdoing it, you could see him behind Landa or the other characters in the sketch, and on more than one occasion, when he was barely visible in the scene, he'd say that his profile had been obscured by the shadows. He would always tell us that, for an artist, there was nothing more constructive than self-criticism." The soundtrack of the highway incorporated the sound of a river. The road was narrow and bumpy. The road's shoulders had weakened from torrential downpours in the past. On some stretches, drivers had to judge visually who could squeeze past first, in order to prevent the car from going over the edge. The road to Altamira was a steep ascent. "And your old lady?" Luis asked, "what did she see in someone like him? You don't talk much about her." Bob Dylan: "Absolutely Sweet Marie." Vadier, curled up in one corner of the back of the car, was snoring loudly and rhythmically.

"Eugenia's a sad case," I replied, staring at a distant waterfall. "They met in the mid-eighties. She was in the theater in Las Palmas and, as far as I know, was involved in setting up something called The Artist's House. But in some way, Eugenia always knew she'd be a failure in the theater. She rehearsed at night, and took Human Resources classes at the Institute of Industrial Technology during the day." "What the fuck is Human Resources?" "How should I know, a career." "And what does a fucker who graduates from Human Resources do?" "No idea. All I know is that a 'humanresourcer' is better off than an actor is. In general, artists are hard up for money. The fact is that Eugenia met my old man in that crazy world of theater and television. I don't know what she saw in him, but, apparently, she fell in love. Three months later she was pregnant with Daniel. They got married and were unhappy ever after. My mom got work at Tamayo." "What's Tamayo?" "I'm not sure. A company that imports booze, I think. After Daniel was born, she left the madness of the theater behind. In contrast to Alfonso, Eugenia was quite embarrassed by her show-business past. The few things she had on VHS tape, she deleted. For the sake of my mental health and Daniel's, she destroyed the photos and videos in which she appeared making a fool of herself. Have you ever heard of a soap opera called *Abigaíl*?" "Wasn't that dumbass Carrillo in that show?" It began to drizzle. Little by little, the cold seeped into my bones. "I think so, I'm not sure. My mom acted in that shit." "Really? How cool!" he said, smiling. "Well, let's just say she appeared in it, rather than acted in it. *Abigaíl*, from what I've been told, was set in a prep school. There were about twenty characters in it: the female lead, her friends at the school, and ten or twelve other girls who were bit players. In some scenes, to make the schoolyard look full, they'd put in a few extra useless girls. My mom was one of those useless girls." Vadier woke up. He drew up his head like a dog and belched. "Where's my Maigualida?" he said with the lines of a tire jack etched across his cheek.

"Where the fuck is Vadier?" Luis had asked a few minutes before leaving the motel. He entered the room, saw blood and broken glass. He didn't flinch. Besides, he didn't bother asking about the state of my bloodied foot. He slammed the door. Bastard, I said to myself. I had the distinct impression that his little speech about love the other day, the one that had made me dance like the dumbest Teletubby, had just been a "performance." Vadier wasn't in the back of the Fiorino. Luis looked all over for him in that dump of a motel. I went down to the grocery store, which had just raised its roller shutters, and asked the Portuguese Creole if he'd seen my friend. The "tri-polar" had apparently disappeared. Luis, in a foul mood, decided to leave him behind in Barinas. He started up the Fiorino and left the keys to the room in the key-deposit box outside reception. "Fuck!"

he said abruptly. For the first time that day he looked me in the eye. "Did you tell me he made friends with some fat woman or did I make it up?" In a low voice, I told him that I had. "That son of a bitch," he replied. "Where does the fat lady live? That guy can't see some fat chick without going crazy over her. He's got to be around here somewhere." The reception door was locked. However, a small open window looked into the house. Luis laced his fingers together and, using his hands as a stirrup, hoisted me up. Holding onto a flimsy security grille, I tried to get a peek inside. The place was dark. It was very quiet. "Vadier, you rat!" Luis whispered, "we're leaving!" With a gesture of his hand, he urged me to take part in calling out to him. "Vadier," I whispered, "Vadier, it's late. Let's get going!" "Ring the bell," Luis said. "Fuck, this is bullshit. That fat woman, Maigualida, must be sleeping. Besides, there are like twelve kids who live in this house." "Son of a bitch!" he replied. "Vadier, you little faggot, we're leaving!" he yelled louder. "Honk the horn," I suggested as a last resort. He looked at me with contempt: "Jeez, Eugenia, haven't you even noticed?" "What?" "The horn in the Fiorino doesn't work." We spent the next five minutes waiting and calling out to him. Suddenly, the door opened. Vadier came out hugging a pillow. His eyes were red and oozing goop. Stashed down his trunks, like a thug's gun, was a bottle of Blue Label. He walked like a zombie, zigzagging toward the Fiorino. "What's up, rats?" he said. He opened the back door, and dived in headfirst into the back of the car. That, at least, made Luis regain his smile.

After rounding a gravelly curve, we saw the first sign: "Altamira de Cáceres, 1 mile." The arrow pointed to the right. The Fiorino took an incline. The sound of cascading water, along with Dylan's harmonica, seemed like the chords of a popular song. Six hours later I would learn that Laurent Blanc had found a gateway to Hell.

2

Old age is evidence of God's duplicity. What the years do to the body is a tasteless act. Time, in slow motion, bestows blemishes, gray hairs, wrinkles; the mirror becomes a sadist. Insomnia gives rise to hyperrealistic images in which I appear as deaf, bald, wearing dentures and the blank stare of someone with inoperable cataracts. Euthanasia should be offered as a humane alternative to senility. I've never liked old people. I could never live with the knowledge that a simple sneeze or a pain in the chest is a close brush with death. Incapacity also scares me to death. The day that someone has to wipe my ass, I will demand my right to reply. My whole life has been one long anticipation of things that haven't happened yet, an exaggerated rendering of what's to come, of what lies ahead. I know I won't be able to bear it when what I want is transformed into what I wanted, when what I aspire to is confused with what I aspired to, when existence becomes nothing more than an endless reproach, a complaint against expired dreams. I'm convinced that, in the end, when it's time to take stock, I will be dissatisfied. I think the most difficult thing in life is maintaining the concerted effort involved in being happy. Happiness has always been a myth, something that happens to others. Happiness only happened to me on the highway leading out of Caracas, in Barinas, in Mérida, and, despite the bitter pill I had to swallow, in the ghost town of Altamira. That weekend things wandered off script.

An old man, who looked to be a hundred and an intolerable drunk, was lying down on a bench in the square. Beyond that scrawny geriatric, who tried in vain to get up, Altamira seemed like a ghost town. Even the wind seemed careful to be quiet; the leaves shuffled around in the emptiness. "Where does your grandfather live?" Luis asked. "No fucking idea. At Herminia's house, I suppose." "And how do we find Herminia's house?" he asked. I shrugged my shoulders. "Who's Herminia?" Vadier cut in. "What are we doing in this little town?" Luis was irritable. He responded to me—when he did respond—with reluctance and snooty laughter. We walked down narrow blocks. It wasn't an ugly place. In contrast to the other small towns we'd passed through, Altamira had a vague charm. It was clean. There were no dirty gutters littered with trash or corner stores besieged by miserable wretches. The drunk on the park bench, who hadn't managed to get up during the fifteen minutes we spent wandering through the narrow streets, was a harmless character. Nor did we find the usual lowlife trading folk songs or sexy salsa at full volume with armed and narrow-minded neighbors. The walls—the majority of them white—were streaked with rust-colored water stains. There were also houses painted baby blue, apple green, and canary yellow. There were no posters of politicians or ugly graffiti. The largest building was a school, whose name I've forgotten. "This shitty place looks like Forks, the town in *Twilight*. This is where Cullen's poor cousins must live. Good thing it's early. If we'd arrived any later, we'd end up as midnight snacks for vampires," Vadier said. We walked in silence. "You watch, any minute now a ghost will appear. If you see some little kid thumbing a ride when we leave, just ignore

did you come? What did you want—to get laid? You're a fucking whore…" Taking my cue from the traditional, over-the-top example of the local soap operas, I slapped him across the face. However, breaking with pre-established scenarios, the leading man didn't grab me and kiss me forcefully. I'm not sure why, but moments before hitting him, I stretched out my hand. When he went crazy and began to insult me, I clenched my fist. I know I hit him hard. The blow clammed him up. If I'd punched him on the nose with my knuckles—as I'd first planned on doing—he would've had to be carried out of Altamira on a stretcher. "What's wrong with you, you jerk? Shut your mouth," I said to him. I don't know how I managed to fake composure. Natalia always said that the thickness in my voice could unnerve even the bravest of truckers. My pretense of calmness managed to intimidate him. "I came to this shithole because *you* wanted me to. You were the one who insisted I come with you. Don't you remember? You asked me to come because you wanted to butt fuck Samuel Lauro." After that, he let loose with a string of expletives, of which I can only recall the lame word "whore." "Listen, Luis Tévez"— subconsciously, I employed the melodramatic national strategy during marital arguments of calling him by his full name —"if you call me a whore again, I'll kill you." I grabbed the anti-theft device from the Fiorino, puffed out my chest, and struck it against the ground twice. "Guys, guys!" Vadier cried out; a jovial, friendly cry, "I think I've found Herminia's house." Ctrl-Alt-Del. Rage and doubt swapped places. "Come on, let's go," Vadier said, tapping my shoulder, and in a low voice (a very low voice), added: "Don't pay any attention to him. I'll talk to him later." We went about half a block, and Vadier pointed to a broad, thick wall

of the bodega as a new pupil. "If you go to Caracas, you'll see how the range of ice cream has been degraded. If you're looking for normal ice cream, you won't find any; you'll find moronic ones like *Stracciatella*, which is nothing more than vanilla with chocolate. Or failing that, *Fior di latte*, which is also vanilla with chocolate but with more vanilla than chocolate. And what about strawberry? Strawberry has been prostituted into a thousand flavors with unpronounceable names, with an aesthetic ridicule that is clearly unacceptable." "Vadier!" I begged. "It's the truth, Eugenia, don't get mad. EFE brand ice creams should regain their monopoly of the market. I think that Ice Cream Rights should exist." Carlos Varela went back to the counter. "Are you from Caracas?" he asked in a hollow voice. What a strange man, I said to myself. I didn't know whether to trust him or not. He didn't seem to be menacing, but he did give off a certain vile stench and a feeling of indefinable perversion. "Yes," I replied. "And where are you heading?" Luis entered the bodega. He still had that childish, angry look on his face. I ignored his presence. "We're heading to Mérida," I said awkwardly, "although, in reality, we're looking for someone here in Altamira. We're looking for Señora Herminia." Carlos Varela let go of the rag in his hands and stepped aside from the ice cream machine. "Herminia's not here right now. She's in Santo Domingo with the group. She'll be back later this afternoon," he said. He seemed to salivate anxiously. His dead eyes pierced through my blouse. What group? I wondered to myself. The atmosphere became strange. Carlos took out a battered-looking calculator. His fingers were long and calloused. He punched the keys of the calculator with unnecessary force. I assumed he must be an oaf; working out the bill for two cups of ice cream didn't require any particular arithmetic agility. Vadier paid for the ice creams. Uncertainty led me to make the following comment. "I'm not actually looking for Herminia; I'm looking for a person who supposedly lives with her." Carlos Varela frowned. Then, he let out a strange laugh. "I'm looking for my grandfather, Laurent Blanc." "Who?" he replied immediately. "Laurent Blanc," I repeated. An awkward silence hung in the air. "I don't know him. I've never heard that name before." "I was told he lives at Señora Herminia's house. This is her house, isn't it?" "Yes, dear, it is. But if there's someone by the name of Laurent Blanc living here, then he must be hiding in the basement. I've lived here for the past fifteen years, and I can assure you that I've never heard of him."

"What the hell is wrong with you, Luis?" I said to him without anger. He was leaning against a white rock, smoking. The water cascaded down in front of us, splashing our ankles. He didn't respond. However, he gave me a sympathetic wink. He took my hand, let it go; picked it back up, and once again, let it go. He walked toward the mountain. At the time, we were in a picturesque village called Calderas, a remote hamlet about fifteen minutes from Altamira. Despite my misgivings, which remained unclassifiable, Carlos Varela had become our guide. The proprietor of the bodega insisted that we wait for his wife, Herminia. "There must be an explanation," he said. He mentioned something about a group and a get-together whose motive was unclear. "Altamira is empty," Carlos had said. "Many people, taking advantage of the holiday season, prefer to go to Santo Domingo or to Apartaderos to sell handicrafts, local food, and cheat unsuspecting tourists out of their money." Carlos was in his mid-forties but seemed much younger. He had curly hair and a big nose. A few days later, Vadier would describe Carlos Varela as the living dead. Without totally agreeing with my wicked friend, I have to say that the proprietor-cum-guide was a bit of a cold fish; his arms were smooth and completely hairless. He didn't have many eyelashes either, and his eyebrows looked like they were painted on. The funny thing was that, although his behavior made us feel reticent, at the same time it inspired confidence in us. Carlos Varela told us that he organizes agritours to mountain resorts. That day, due to a severe headache, he had decided to remain in Altamira. As a result, it was Herminia who drove the group instead. "They're easy trips," he said. "We walk to the waterfalls of Santo Domingo, go see a few lagoons, and sometimes we even go as far as Calderas. People from Caracas are easily deceived. It's an easy trail, a simple route. If you use the word 'agritourism' or 'eco-tourism,' people believe that it's some fancy, exclusive route or one sponsored by some NGO. People from Caracas are generally pretty gullible." I suppose that kind of cynical argument pleased Luis and Vadier. Honestly, I don't know why we decided to humor him and let him take us to that inhospitable village.

"Do you have any plans for the afternoon?" the shopkeeper had asked. I said nothing. Vadier said that he'd do whatever we wanted. Luis played dumb. "I could take you to see the Calderas waterfalls; there's some very nice scenery worth seeing." "I'm sorry, Carlos, but we don't have any money," I remarked with a frown. "Don't worry about that. I wouldn't do it for money. I must admit, I'm also curious about the story of your grandfather, the tenant." I didn't

He put his fingers under my chin. "You're gonna realize that I'm not worth shit, that's all." We stood beside the rock for a while. We looked like two characters in a movie poster for a bad film, an eighties melodrama with Tom Cruise and some wooden actress who, years later, would end up as an extra on *Lost* or on *Desperate Housewives.* "I'm gonna ruin everything, Princess. I always mess up." "Why do you have to ruin anything? Fuck, Luis, what's the matter? Enough with all the tragedy. How silly you are!" I sought out his mouth. Our lips met briefly, but his didn't stay on mine. "You'll find out that I'm a jerk, you'll see." "I know that you're a jerk, and I don't care. As if I'm any better. What's the problem? I'm not worth shit either. I came to this ghost town to find a guy who doesn't exist. My life is a joke, Luis, but what the hell. Why should I care that you're not worth shit? Besides, whose life is worth anything anyway?" He raised his head and pulled me closer to him. Not in a sleazy reggaeton way. My sensibility collapsed. Slowly, he thrust his open hand into my hair, then expertly moved it to the back of my neck, guiding my face toward him; his breath hit my lips, our noses rubbed. With Jorge—my only lover—everything had been physical, too physical. I liked kissing him with my eyes open while silently making fun of his stupid face. With Jorge, all things had a particular form and taste; I always felt nauseous from the texture of his tongue and irritated from his bitter saliva, which went straight to the corners of my mouth. My high school romance has always been complicated by a predefined morbidity. Neither with Jorge, nor with anyone else ever again, did I experience anything like what happened on the white rock in Calderas. Oblivious to everything around me, my eyes remained closed. My entire body, wet and throbbing, weightless, seemed to be dissolving in acid. In slow motion, I felt him bite at my lower lip. The tip of his tongue touched my gum. He pulled his mouth away from mine and gave me a gentle peck on the forehead. His lips remained there for what seemed like an eternity—how awful that word "eternity" is. Nevertheless, I have to admit that that embrace, although it lasted only three minutes, seemed to go on forever. A few days later, when I toned down the rosy hue of my romance, Vadier would tell me there was no need to feel ashamed, since the only sensible thing people did in the world was make the effort to love each other. Luis's right hand was on my waist, his fingers on the thin fabric of my T-shirt seemed like a container of dry ice. Love—I understood that day—is nothing more than a deep sense of surrender. I've always been quite selfish: me first, me second, me third, and so on until infinity. In Calderas, I was convinced that love is nothing more than the monumental breakdown of selfishness. It's easy to joke about these kinds of things when the infection doesn't strike us and when the disease attacks others. Happy people, in these situations, seem stupid, ridiculous; pet names or caresses in public places earn our deepest scorn. For years, I was a harsh critic of displays of affection. However, that week, everything changed. Luis Tévez gave me a strain of Influenza A that, for a long time, made every effort to destroy me. "Forgive me for what I said this morning. I don't know what happened. I messed up," he said, kissing my shoulders. I never imagined that he would ask my forgiveness. An apology was something too predictable. "If you ever call me a whore again, I'll kill you," I said, fixated on his lips. "And you'd do well," he added.

In the end, our deep kiss finally happened. His tongue, by mutual agreement, went down my throat; a thin, warm tongue, with slight and constant twists; his lips pressed tightly against mine. (Jorge, in general, just slobbered all over me.) His high waist exerted pressure against my stomach; my breasts swelled and pressed against his chest. His left hand, resting on the top of my head, let go of my hair and slowly moved down my back. The natural thing would be to say that he put his hand on my ass, but it's also necessary to add that there are many ways for someone to put his hand on your ass. And that touch, in particular, was sublime. That touch inflamed me. His tongue slipped out of my mouth and installed itself on my neck. A mechanical sound—a kind of "click"—interrupted our late-night movie parody. "Hey, do you guys mind if I watch?" said a familiar voice that forced an abrupt landing. Vadier had one of Luis's cameras slung around his neck. I suddenly became aware of the whole physical situation: saliva, bad breath, teeth, sore throat. Giggling like fools, our mouths collided. Vadier repeated his question: "Do you mind if I watch? I like being a spectator." "You great big motherfucker, Vadier!" Luis said menacingly. I walked off uncomfortably, all sticky and wet. When Luis let go of me, I had a funny feeling, as if a dam had burst inside me. "No, no. Don't mind me, go on, go on," said the voyeur. Luis took me by the hand, and we walked through the cobblestone streets. Vadier, leaping ahead of us like a dog, expounded useless theories about the origin of the world. We followed the trail of smoke. We arrived at a kind of cabin near the last pool of water. Carlos had prepared *choripanes*. "How many do you want?" said the enigmatic host. It was about four o'clock in the afternoon.

3

Herminia was a young woman; adult, but young. I was expecting someone much older, a hundred-year-old crone. If my grandfather actually lived in that town, I had imagined his place of residence would be something like a nursing home. Herminia arrived home in a van filled with people: a fat woman who looked like a dyke, a married couple in their thirties, and two or three others, among whom I recall a bug-eyed brunette. Luis, Vadier, and I were waiting for her in the square, beside the sleeping drunk. When the van arrived, I saw Carlos Varela speak to his wife. She screwed up her face after being questioned, seemingly confused. She walked over slowly and greeted us with studied politeness. She asked me bluntly who I was looking for. I repeated the name of my grandfather once more, a name that meant nothing to her. She scrutinized me. Suddenly, she let out an exclamation. The expression on her face implied that she'd solved the riddle. "Oh, but of course! You're Alfonsito's daughter, isn't that right?" *Alfonsito*, I said to myself. Ridiculous diminutives exist, but without doubt, the one for my father takes the cake. She turned her back to us and called out to Carlos: "She's Alfonso's daughter!" The proprietor nodded, smiling. He seemed to understand as well. Vadier and Luis threw me questioning looks. "Come on, come into the house," said Herminia with a forced smile. "You'll meet Laurent shortly," she said to me in a low voice, pulling me aside. She seemed to be teasing, but without malice, as if she was handling some delicate information. On entering the house, we heard the sounds of a waterfall, birds, and strange animals. Vadier told me the fat woman who looked like a dyke had put on a meditation CD. "Princess," Luis said in a

low voice, "what's all this madness? Who are these people?"
"I don't know," I said. "Eugenia!" Herminia called out from
the bottom of a staircase, "come upstairs with me. I have
something for you." In the middle of the courtyard, the
group from the van lit several incense sticks and sat down
in a circle.

We climbed up to the second floor. I entered a shabby,
dust-filled room lit by an old lamp. Herminia opened an old
dresser drawer. She handed me an envelope with familiar
handwriting that said: *For Eugenia Blanc.* My hand shook.
"Take your time, I'll wait for you downstairs," she added.
She left the room. I remained alone. I opened the envelope
with patient anxiety. In addition to a handwritten letter, I
found a moth-eaten French passport that had expired in 1972
and an ID card from the École Normale Supérieure for the
class of '67–68. The documents belonged to my grandfather,
Laurent Blanc. The black-and-white photo showed a man
who looked like Alfonso; a type of Alfonso with hepatitis.
In the middle of the room was a hammock. I sat down on it
and began to read. From the first few lines, I felt sure that
those words would turn my life to shit.

4

Eugenia,

*Your grandfather had an appliance store in Chacao. In the
late seventies, he started up a company with a man named Pedro,
who disappeared overnight with all the money, even taking the
petty cash. Your grandfather had a nasty temper. My communication with him was about as fluid as ours. I don't know where
in the world my father is. The last time I spoke with him, he was
drunk. He told me that he'd found a gateway to Hell, that he*

intended to tell the world to take a hike and then go off to meet the devil.

Eugenia, with this letter I aim to do what Laurent never did. I want to give you an explanation. I want to try to justify the unjustifiable or try to win, if not your forgiveness, then at least your understanding about certain events.

Herminia Díaz is good person. She helped me to go on when I felt I couldn't do so anymore; when I had finally accepted that my existence was worthless. Herminia organizes live-in group therapy sessions. I know that all this will seem stupid to you, a hobby for people who don't know how to live and who get together to talk about their miseries. I know that you think I'm a failure. In all honesty, I've given you no reason to think otherwise. What little stability I've achieved is thanks to these people, who listened to me, helped me, and gave me an opportunity. And, Eugenia, that's all I'm asking from you: an opportunity. All I ask is that you read the whole letter, that you don't throw it in the bin. After having made such a long journey to the picturesque streets of Altamira, let me tell you a few things. That's all I ask.

It's been very difficult being your father. You have an imposing and intimidating character. I never knew how to talk to you. Your mother doesn't know how to talk to you either, and for all I know, nor did Daniel. Your air of superiority always bothered me. Your look often told those of us who knew you that the way we've faced up to the world is ridiculous and superficial. Maybe you're right.

Your mother and I did whatever we could to give you kids the best. It didn't work, I know. You can't imagine how difficult it was making an effort to pay for your school. That effort destroyed our marriage. Your mother had a regular income. Whereas at that time, I only brought home paltry amounts at the end of each month. Your mother wanted you and your brother to have a good education—a Catholic one, moreover. It was all the same to me. I'd rather have enrolled you in an ordinary and inexpensive school; a place where you would simply spend the mornings. Your mother imposed her will. Almost all of your primary education and that of your brother was a huge burden on her part. Eugenia sacrificed many things, which for me were non-negotiable. Eugenia stopped dreaming to give you and your brother an opportunity. She adapted to the real world while I continued inventing stories in which nobody believed. We always tried to make sure that you and your brother lacked for nothing, that you had the clothes you wanted, that you never went without food, that you had the latest cell phone, the latest music device. Eugenia and I poured all our efforts into helping you and your brother, but it's clear that, at some point, something went wrong. We never lived up to it. I never listened to you, I never listened to your brother. At the age of thirty-three, I continued thinking like a child.

Eventually, I turned out to be just like Laurent. And if there's one thing I swore in life, it's that I wouldn't end up becoming like him. Your grandfather was a very selfish man. My mother and I were liabilities to him. He lashed out all his frustrations on us, his feelings of inferiority as a second-rate European. Laurent studied anthropology in Paris, but never graduated. He put on airs of being erudite and intellectual. I had no grounds on which to question him or expose him as a phony intellectual. He came to America in 1968. He supposedly received a scholarship to undertake a study on anthropometrics at the Mexico Summer Olympics. He never went back to France. I don't know how or when he came to Venezuela. I know he had serious problems at some universities. Apparently, he plagiarized research papers and presentations. He had better luck in Caracas. His French surname and his expired credentials from European universities opened the doors to insti-

tutions that, as a rule, despise the Perezes, the Gonzaleses, the Lópezes, and many others who've completed studies in this country. Laurent was a troublesome man. His temper caused him to fall out with others at the academy. Eventually, after some weird agreement, he started up the appliance business with Old Pedro—the only friend of his I remember—who ripped him off overnight.

After that, Laurent just cleared off. He was there when I married Eugenia. Then, when Daniel was three months old, he showed up at our house. The last time I saw him, you were one and a half years old. I remember you bit one of his fingers. Some Christmases, he'd call up drunk, mumbling things, asking after your grandmother—who died from diabetes in nineteen eighty-something—and, before hanging up, he'd criticize everything about me. The last time we spoke was after what happened to Daniel. He called from Peru. He was either drunk or stoned, I'm not sure which. He'd just learned from a friend that his grandson had died. That's the day he said he would tell the world to take a hike, and then go off to meet the devil. That's all I can tell you about him. I don't know much more. This is the man whose surname could save you. Believe me, if I could have swapped my French surname for one belonging to a person who would have shown me simple affection, I would have done so without hesitation. But at this moment, another surname would be of no use to us. If Laurent's surname can be of any help to you, then let it be so. This is one of the reasons for this letter, Eugenia. Let me help you. Let me do something for you.

I know you can never forgive me for what happened that afternoon. I go over what happened every day of my life. My conscience has become my worst enemy. Just thinking that I could have hurt you—more than I already have hurt you—creates horrible images in my mind that don't let me sleep. If it weren't *for Herminia's group, I don't believe I'd be telling you any of this. All I can say is: that man wasn't me. I was alone, desperate, and distraught. Have you ever had a sudden attack of desperation? Once again, it's not a justification, I just simply want to tell you how I felt at the time and how I feel about it now. Not even God could forgive what I did, for which, I imagine, one day I will meet up with your grandfather again.*

I kept thinking about what you told me about your French nationality. I think I can help you. Tracing it from here will be difficult, but there are other ways to go about it. I'm currently working at the Ministry of Culture. My office is in the Ateneo Cultural Center. It's never been easier to earn money doing so little. This is what I suggest you do: have a look on the internet for something that interests you, a career, a specialization, a course. I can easily get you a scholarship from the Ayacucho Foundation. In principle, you would be given a student visa. Then while you're in France, using Laurent's documents and tracing the surname, it might be easier to process the nationality. I have friends in the Foreign Ministry. I will provide you with all the necessary means to do what you want, so you can get away from this sick country. Think about it, and let me know your decision. You don't know how happy you made me the day you sent me that message, the day we met at the bar in El Rosal.

I wish it were easy to tell you what my life has been like. I hope you don't judge me too harshly. The look in your eyes is very cruel. I always felt that you made fun of me, that my view of the world seemed childish and ridiculous to you. I never told you that the first bit of money I brought home—during one of Laurent's long absences—I won by singing at a local bar. Then a producer took me to RCTV, where I took part in various competitions. That's where I met your mother. We had many dreams, Eugenia. Today, when

I see her, when I talk to her, I ask myself how it was even possible in the first place for us to consider living together as a couple. I imagine that Eugenia asks herself the same thing. Sometimes I think that I'm her deepest regret. I would even say that the coldness that Eugenia projects onto you—and that she projected onto Daniel— has to do with me. When Eugenia looks at you, she sees me as well, and that probably strengthens her bitterness.

We've been done over and used by many people. Eventually, I managed to get a stable job at Venevisión, but by then, your mom already had a good job. She was earning three times as much money as me. She soon fell for another guy. As for me, being thirty-something years old, I kept thinking that one day I would be famous, that I would have the lead role in a soap opera, that I would win a Gold Meridian or a Ronda—stupid awards that have long since disappeared—or that I would have a successful pop song on the radio. I had blind faith in a talent that I exaggerated, and with which I deceived myself for a long time. A talent in which my mother believed and that at one point had captivated Eugenia, but which time has taken care to put firmly in its place. I became the laughing stock of all my colleagues. However, what hurt me most was something you said about me. One day, a supposed record producer offered me the chance to be part of a compilation album. I had a cold at the time. I came up with the idea of inviting him over to the house to show him a terrible video of me appearing in a contest. From the beginning, your mom told me that those people were just pulling my leg. Nevertheless, I believed them. I had to pay to secure an interview with another phantom producer. They came to the house four or five times to see the video. Not long after, someone told me they did it just to get laughs, that they met up in a bar to dream up pranks. But what hurt me most was to hear you and Daniel say that I embarrassed you. You said you were sorry that I took you to school. I came into your room and looked into your eyes, do you remember? Daniel got all nervous and left. You looked me up and down and asked me what I wanted. You've had that severe and implacable gaze ever since you were a little girl. It's true, Eugenia, my life hasn't been great. I bet on something and lost. I had an opportunity and I let it go by. I had two wonderful children, and I never got to know them. One died, and the other hates me. I hope you never commit the same errors I did. If you need it, Herminia can help you. I know you won't talk to her. I'm sure she appears to you as a ridiculous person running a help group for fools. Milagros, a friend of hers, works with adolescents in Caracas. I know that she could be more useful to you than that little doctor of yours, Fragachán, who your mother takes you to every two weeks at the cost of more than five hundred dollars. Have you ever wondered how much Fragachán costs or, for that matter, what the preparatory course on Saturday costs? Do you know that your mom refused a job offer in Bogotá because she thought that the move would hurt Daniel, because she thought the best thing for you was to remain with your old friends? Life is difficult, Eugenia. It's easy to criticize and judge when you don't have to make any sacrifices. Don't be so hard on your mom. I know that she's a difficult person, but I can assure you that, at one time, she was a charming woman, full of life and dreams for you and your brother, for us, for our frustrated professions. We failed. I failed. In this country, the natural thing is to lose. For that reason, daughter, I understand why you want to leave, to try your luck in another place. Go, Eugenia. You will have all my support. I think it's a very wise decision. This country is fucked, it's finished. Get out and try to do something with your life in a normal place.

I've told you many things, and yet I have the feeling that I haven't told you anything. Forgive me for tricking you this way, for making up Altamira. I felt it was the only way for me to reach you. "A journey unlocks the doors to one's heart," I read in an almanac once. That's why it occurred to me to take advantage of your decision to find your grandfather, in order to tell you something. I know that besides doors, your heart has bars, locks, gates, and a surveillance system. I hope somehow, even if it was only for a moment, you let me reach you. Not a day goes by that I don't think of you. Not a day goes by that I don't feel regret. Not a day goes by that I don't feel the terrible urge to start all over again, to begin my life afresh from the moment when a nurse placed Daniel in my hands, or when, much later, you arrived during a complicated cesarean. I know this will seem ridiculous and trite to you, but I have to say it. This is what I felt: you were the most beautiful baby girl I had ever seen; you had the biggest eyes, for which I felt a genuine and immense sense of pride. After that, Eugenia, I don't know what happened. Everything was lost. I've had a shitty life. I lost you, I hurt you, I left, only to come back one awful afternoon to turn into your worst nightmare. If you've come this far, thank you for listening to me—for reading me. I haven't told you everything I wanted to tell you, but in a way, I feel free.

Think about your future, and let me know what you decide. Included with this letter are two of Laurent's documents. They were the only things I found. I'm sorry you didn't get to meet your grandfather. I hope that the meeting with me hasn't been a disappointment. I wish you all the blessings of the world. Look after yourself. Count on me for whatever you need. For now, at least, I know that I can help you out financially. I know you hate sentimentality. I hope you don't judge me or criticize me for saying openly that I love you and that I hope that, one day, you can look me in the face without feeling fear, contempt, or pity.

Your dad, A.

MOORLAND MALADY

1

"You drive, Princess, I don't feel so good," Luis said. He lay down in the back of the Fiorino. The sky wasn't blue or gray or white; it seemed like a sky with anemia. Vadier was chatting with Maigualida. My neck hurt. A restless night had aggravated my scoliosis. I'd slept in a fetal position, anticipating a forceps delivery and preeclampsia. Morning brought about the transformation: Luis decided to shut himself up inside his own bubble, impenetrable, intractable, intolerable. I woke up enclosed in his arms, using his shoes as a pillow. We had spent the night in the Fiorino. Our escape from Altamira had led us back to Barinitas. Darkness, a broken headlight, and the fog were arguments in favor of the return. In the end, Barinitas was only twenty-five minutes from Altamira. On the road, trucks and drunks put Luis's reflexes to the test. From what he told me, his migraine had erupted behind his right eye. When we arrived at Maigualida's motel, the gate was closed. However, the sound of a merengue—Elvis Crespo belting out

"Paint Me"— invited us to enter through the side door. The fat woman greeted us affectionately. She told us that, unfortunately, the motel was full that night, but that she could open the gate so we could park our car inside. She gave us each a beer and invited us inside her house, where they were celebrating some random guy's birthday. Luis's head was burning. His temples were throbbing. He tried bringing down the fever by rubbing the cold can of beer against his forehead. The light hurt his eyes. "Damned highway," he said. In my backpack—probably expired—I found two aspirins. He took them and went to lie down. Vadier and I hung out at the fat woman's house for a while. Neither of us mentioned anything about what had happened in Altamira. When we returned to the Fiorino, we found Luis in the back seat listening to "Visions of Johanna." He was holding his head in both hands and tracing circles at his temples with his thumbs. We didn't talk much that night. There were no jokes, no grand lectures on useless matters, no plausible explanations about our escape. Vadier stretched out in the passenger seat. Luis and I lay down in the back. I slept dreamlessly: a black background, impregnable. All of a sudden, light appeared. I opened my eyes clumsily; the world was out of focus and without form. My back ached, and I had a crick in my neck. My right hand was numb. In my transit to the world, I encountered Luis's gaze. In vain I tried to touch his face with my hand, but he seemed to have a phobia toward me. Damned wretch. I didn't know how to deal with his personality changes. Luis Tévez made me feel like a yo-yo. Besides which, Alfonso's words rubbed salt and alcohol in every one of my wounds. "What's the matter, Luis?" I asked him in a low voice. Vadier let out a

the aim of transforming them into strengths. "Get me out of here, please!" I begged Luis after suffering an attack of desperation and intolerance. "It's late, Princess. It's dark," he said calmly. "The Fiorino has a broken headlight. Striking out for Mérida now would be madness. Unless..." "Go on, say it, whatever, it doesn't matter." "Unless we go back to Barinitas," he said, completing his thought. Carlos Varela put on a CD by Enya. The "initiates" invited us to close their circle. In the background, Vadier began playing clapping games with the bug-eyed brunette. That son of a bitch, I said to myself after hearing him sing: "L for lime, O for orange, V for violet, E for emerald: that signifies passionate love." The strangest thing, though, was his genuine smile. "Do you want anything?" asked Herminia, who suddenly appeared at my side, adding that she would fix up one of the rooms so we could spend the night. I told her we appreciated the gesture but explained that some friends were expecting us in Barinitas. "How are you?" she asked, scrutinizing me as if I were a little girl. "Fine," I answered without feeling, merely out of courtesy. "Do you want to talk?" "No thanks. I don't want to talk right now." She remained by my side for a while. She told me the house had been in her family for many years. Her mother—Herminia—was confined to a hospital in Mérida with severe memory problems. "Your mother has the same name as you, too, isn't that right? What a coincidence!" she said to me. I cursed Alfonso, I cursed my naivety. I flashed a false smile. I faked a coughing fit and turned my back to her. In the central courtyard, the group's discussion was starting to sound like party conversation. Carlos Varela handed out pens and paper to each of the participants. Vadier, who appeared as though he'd known everyone since he was a kid, got up after recounting a joke and asked Luis for the keys to the Fiorino. Luis, quite confused by his surroundings, searched for them in his pocket and threw them to him. "What's up with you, Princess? What did the letter say?" he asked, annoyed. I didn't have time to reply. The party broke up moments later, when Vadier returned to the courtyard and placed a bottle of Blue Label on the table. "This party's really great," he said, "but it's bone dry." Then he turned to Carlos Varela and asked, "Hey, dead man, do you want a mass?" A church-like silence fell over the group. The bug-eyed brunette covered her face with her hands. Herminia came running out and covered the bottle with a towel. "What's wrong?" Vadier asked. The thirty-year-old married woman began to cry and ran off toward one of the rooms. Carlos Varela went white as a sheet. "Luis, please, get me out of here," I begged, dragging him into the street. We had to wait for Vadier in the Fiorino for about fifteen minutes. He was choking with laughter when he got back to the car. After this drama, his friend, the brunette, told him that the group therapy meeting was a joint session with AA members. After that weekend in Altamira, they were supposed to take stock of the past twelve months they'd spent without touching any alcohol. Unbeknown to us, that bottle of Blue Label undid months of therapy and psychoanalysis. Vadier told us that, when he became aware of the disaster, he apologized. Herminia told him not to worry, but clearly, the damage had been done. All the "initiates" went back to their rooms. The Fiorino took off under the night sky. When we came to the sign announcing the turnoff to Santo Domingo, a little boy was thumbing a ride. Vadier stopped laughing. He crossed

serve as a badge of identity, and for some people it strikes a pose in their photographic album of time. For example, I know that Bob Dylan wrote "Visions of Johanna" for Luis. Well, that's true in my universe, and at the end of the day, that's all that matters to me. For his part, Vadier is a "random playlist." A blend of ballads, pop, fusion, etc. The Trans-Andean Highway forced us to borrow from a repertoire that has disappeared and that the speed of the century has condemned to the dustbin of history. Luis was right. Those bands—*my* bands—have been consigned to oblivion. Dylan, on the other hand, still has various shrines. Vadier sang songs by Juanes, Alejandro Sanz, and Álex Ubago. He didn't have his own style. He imitated the singers' throaty voices, exaggerating their delivery. I remember, amid winding curves and the gentle breezes of the road, we sang a duet by Alejandro Sanz and Shakira, "Thank You, But No." It was fun. It was his number one track, our most commercial piece. He spun the iPod's wheel with his fingers while shouting out things like, "Awesome stuff, Eugenia!" and "How cool!" Then he pressed "Play," stuck his head out the window, and like a Heidi with gender-identity issues, he sang to the mountain. Luis was asleep in the back of the car. We played many songs. We listened to my favorite track two or three times: "Peter Pan" by El Canto del Loco. Vadier didn't know the song well and only repeated the final chorus. It was cold. Rolling up the windows in the Fiorino wasn't easy and required some strength. Of all the songs on that "road concert," one in particular stands out. Caressing the iPod, Vadier said: "The Fray—'How to Save a Life.' Oh, Eugenia! This is freakin' excellent." The cork dashboard became a piano. He improvised the first few chords. It was a finely

"Maybe, I'm not sure." iPod. Artist>Melendi>*Curiosa la cara de tu padre*>"Un violinista en tu tejado." "I think sex is over-rated," he said. "People have been screwing for over three thousand years at least. Now, though, it seems like it's something new, awesome, a publicity stunt. What a load of shit, Eugenia!" He raised the index finger of his right hand, as if delivering a lecture. "Human beings have sucked an infinite number of dicks and an infinite number of tits." I laughed at his aphorism. "That sounds like a saying in an almanac, by one of those geniuses," I said. "Einstein?" "Yeah, him or Newton or da Vinci or some other pussy." "Some of my friends, this sad sack included," he said, indicating Luis, "probably told you that I'm tri-polar. Those guys like talking out their ass. I'm no fucking tri-polar. Sometimes I lose my head when I'm mixing substances. What I can tell you is that I'm trisexual. I swing every which way. I'm down for whatever." "Trisexual? What the fuck are you talking about?" "Women, men, BDSM, toys. Whatever." "How nasty!" "It's the truth, I like everything. Each has its own charm." "Have you been with guys?" I asked, a bit disgusted but curious all the same. "Yeah, two or three times. It was great!" "But you like girls as well?" "Yeah, some, not all." "Who do you prefer most?" "I like them both equally. Sometimes girls and sometimes guys. It depends on how I'm feeling; it depends on the day and on what I feel like. If I feel like tits, it's girls; and if I feel like ass, then it's guys. Fucking ass can be amazing." "Go on then, explain it to me," I said, smiling to myself. "At first, getting fucked up the ass is great. Most people don't think of it as a part of the body for doing something like that. It hurts a lot, but suddenly, everything changes. The pain turns into pleasure; it's an amazing feeling. Do you

in the absence of a CT scan and any visible signs, I still haven't been made aware of yet. I never would have guessed something like this could happen. Although the situation was somewhat predictable, I wasn't expecting it, not like that. Luis's decision took me by surprise. I think we stopped because we were hungry. I don't remember. He was irritable. Before we pulled up in front of a shop whose facade displayed ponchos, towels, ceramic plaques, and other "faggy" souvenirs—that's how Vadier referred to them—he had demanded we put on the Dylan cassette. Then he said that Melendi was a criminal who deserved to be tried for crimes against music, and that the members of the band La Oreja de Van Gogh were purveyors of nonsense. "What happened in Belgium?" I asked. Vadier ordered a large latte. He lit a cigarette. A cross-eyed little fat guy caught our attention and, addressing us with the formal *usted* form, told us that smoking wasn't permitted. We got out of the car. Vadier bought himself a brown poncho covered in pastel-colored squares. Luis got lost among a multitude of elderly tourists, who were most probably enjoying their last vacation. Sensing my concern, Vadier told me to leave him alone: "Don't mind him; he'll get over it." Love made me fragile. That game of trial and error was wearing me down. I tried to ignore his standoffishness but, inevitably, I felt alienated. "Did you know Lisette?" "Who?" "Lisette," Vadier repeated. "Luis's first girlfriend." "No, never heard of her." "I think she's in Houston or Atlanta now with her family, I'm not sure." Vadier seemed to be talking to himself. He wasn't his usual loudmouth self, joking and full of theories. He looked like a deflated balloon, like a dummy. His glasses were in his hand; there were bits of leaves stuck in his hair, which was still damp from the puddle he'd landed in. "Vadier, what happened in Belgium?"

Luis was sitting on a wooden railing, gazing openly at the promiscuity of the mountain. "And now, little boy, what the hell is wrong with you?" I asked him. I clasped my hands around his neck. He flinched slightly but didn't resist me. "I can't go on like this, putting up with all your shit during the day and then falling into your arms at night. Tell me what's bothering you. What's the problem?" He said nothing. He screwed up his lips and blew out the smoke, as if trying to sketch figures in the air. "I've already told you, Princess. I'm not worth shit. Sooner or later you'll realize that."

"Old Man Armando checked Luis into some sort of psych ward. Luis was hospitalized for about six months. He'd tried to kill himself twice. Besides that, he was addicted to some stuff called Tegretol, or something like that. He swallowed that shit like it was candy."

"Ignore me, Princess. My problem isn't with you. I don't want to mess things up for you. I don't want to hurt you. The best thing you can do is forget about me. I'm not the right guy for you. Jorge's probably much better suited to you." He squirmed out of my embrace. "It's cold, isn't it?" he said. His eyes said nothing. He seemed absent. He looked like a ghost that other ghosts poked fun at. A funny-looking phantom disguised under a white sheet.

"Do you remember what I told you about Prague, the story about the tram?" I nodded in silence. "That was no accident. I'm almost certain that Luis intended to put himself in the path of that shit. I was a numbskull and didn't realize it. Fortunately, Floyd was onto him. When the psychiatrists released him, they said he was fine. Some doctors—so-called European big shots with Spanish surnames—even wrote a report in which they stated that the brain of the young man was repowered. And, to be honest, I thought he was fine. He and Floyd spent a few weeks together in Europe. That's where we met up. He didn't bring up the subject of Lisette, but when that incident with the tram occurred, I thought they must've left him with a few screws loose at the sanatorium in Belgium."

He insisted on his bolero lyrics, on his bleeding-heart rhetoric. "One day you'll realize that I'm a useless deadbeat, you'll go ape and tell me to fuck off. If we let things get more complicated, in the end everything will be worse." "Shut up. If you keep on saying stupid things like that, I'll go ape right now. Drop all this nonsense."

"Lisette was the excuse. Luis went crazy. She was a normal, ordinary girl, cute, with no ass or tits. Luis became obsessed with her. She told him to take a hike, and the dude could think of nothing better to do than put a bullet through his head. It was the first time that Floyd had saved his life. He found Luis holding the gun to his own head. They argued, cursed each other out, and broke into a struggle. In the end, the gun went off. The bullet that Luis intended to put through his head went into his shoulder instead. I'm not sure if you've seen the scar left behind by that bullet wound."

"Why did you ask me to come with you? Didn't you think that this would happen?" I said. "What do you mean by *this*?" he replied, spitting out the final word sarcastically. "You know what I'm referring to." "We came to see your precious little grandfather who doesn't exist. Cut the melodrama. Don't get all soppy." He pushed me awkwardly, clearly looking for a fight. "*This!*" he repeated. "What the fuck is 'this?' There's nothing going on here. We're just friends. I came with you to find your grandfather, and you're meant to come with me to Mérida, where I have some business to take care of. That's it. What you're referring to as 'this' is something you made up, so don't piss me off." "What business do you have to take care of in Mérida?" I asked impassively. Jorge would never have spoken to me in that tone. I would never have let him do it. Luis broke down all my defenses. His attitude made me feel an indescribably painful emptiness. His words—mixed up with those of Alfonso—cut me to the quick. He didn't respond. He shrugged his shoulders contemptuously. Everything was spinning. I couldn't contain my nausea any longer, and in a shrill voice I burst out, "Are you gonna go and suck Samuel Lauro's cock, you asshole?" "What I do with Samuel is not your problem. And get your hand outta my face; you look like a raving hysteric." No one had ever succeeded in making me feel so angry before. We cursed each other out, shooting daggers at one another. My words—mostly barbed—carried venom without an antidote. I called him every name under the sun. He shot back at me with elaborate invectives whose meaning I didn't get. "You're right, you're a pathetic dumbass," I said to him in the end. Then he pointed out my annoying snobbishness, my capacity for selfishness, my phony moods, my two-faced nature. I tried to steady my breathing. I tried to regain control of the situation. Without raising my voice, I slowly backed away. "Luis, let's just drop it for now, OK? What the fuck. We'll talk about this some other time." I went back out onto the street. All of a sudden, after I had recovered my senses, I found myself caught up in a throng of old people who were part of the "Second Chance Tour." A little old lady clutching a walking frame asked me to take her picture standing beside a stone church. Vadier was chatting amiably with some tourists. I wanted to run. I wanted to scream. I wanted to rip all my clothes off in public. But I did nothing. A decrepit old woman stared at me contemptuously, and for a moment, I had the impression that she'd given me the evil eye.

"Señora Aurora lives in a parallel world. The incident with the gun, for example, never happened. She blames Luisito's 'accident' on that 'albino bastard.' Señora Aurora made up the story that Luis went to Belgium to obtain the European Baccalaureate that, clearly, she thought was far superior to these provincial schools here. She described Luis's episodes of depression as just 'temporary ailments,' as 'viruses,' as 'eccentricities' that could be fixed with a game of Wii or PlayStation. It was the same when he took the three boxes of Rivotril. Luisito got 'confused,' he had 'a headache' and thought that they were aspirins. It was all just an accident. That's where all the problems with Armando started. Armando's a real weirdo, a creep, a forty-something-year-old guy who thinks he's still sixteen. To Luis he's a hero, an example, a model person. That's total bullshit, Eugenia! Armando Tévez is nothing more than a rich cokehead who won't man up. But at least Armando acknowledges that Luis has a problem. He found the psych ward in Belgium—don't ask me how—and paid for the best treatment. Besides that, he also paid for Floyd's stay in Europe. Now the old man lives in exile in Costa Rica. They recorded a phone conversation in which he was allegedly conspiring against the government. The warrant for his arrest was issued about five months ago."

Apart from the poncho, Vadier bought himself a pair of gloves and a cap. He blew warm breaths into his hands to ward off the chill. Luis suddenly appeared. He poked fun at Vadier's outfit and started fooling around with a snow globe that simulated falling snow when turned upside down. The geriatrics from the nursing home slowly climbed back aboard their tour bus. And then it happened. Words, gestures, thoughts, sounds quickly formed into a migraine. "Who's up for a hot chocolate?" Vadier asked. Across the street was a huge sign that read CAFÉ. "Sure thing!" Luis said. The winding road was empty. I took a step toward the street. My thoughts felt the net weight of melancholy. I heard murmuring voices, Vadier laughing. I knew that they were following right behind me. "No great loss if I get run over, right?" I heard his faltering voice. I thought it was just a joke. I continued walking with my hands in my pockets; my fingers were frozen. I got to the curb. It took me a while to realize that neither of them was standing next to me. "Move it, dumbass," Vadier shouted. Vadier was about five feet away from me and about ten feet away from Luis, who stood rooted to the spot in the upstream lane. "No, you guys go on ahead, don't mind me. After all, it makes no difference whether one exists or not. I already told you that my life's not worth shit." Hee, hee, ha, ha, I laughed silently to myself. He's just fucking around, I said to myself. The outline of a bus appeared around the bend. "Come on then," I said in a low voice. Vadier's petrified expression made me realize that this wasn't just playacting. "Move it *now*, cocksucker!" he shouted to Luis. Reality appeared to move in slow motion. From the other direction, in the distance, an SUV appeared. Luis's eyes sought out mine. He seemed to be floating above the concrete. Slowly, he crouched down. "I'm staying here," he said. "You guys go." Goddammit! What to think? What to do? Invisible chains bound my feet. I turned into stone, into a pillar of salt—I recalled a religious instruction class in which I heard the story about a woman made of salt. At some point, nightmares become far-fetched. There's a moment in every bad dream when you realize: things like this just don't happen; the absurd circumstances causing you to panic are fantastic in nature. When I heard the SUV's horn, I thought that my nightmare had ended. The bus in the opposite lane flashed its lights. The brakes screeched. I tried to scream. Nothing came out. My lips were clamped tight, on mute. Luis wouldn't budge. Vadier cursed him and shouted things to him. The cold wind tied my wrists together. In a split second, I managed to construct a semi-realistic picture: Luis smashed to pieces, his head rolling toward my feet, his blood staining the snow. Suddenly, his face took on the form of Daniel's face. I found him in his room, doubled over on his knees, with his mouth foaming. The absent gaze was the same: there it was again, that fucking son of a bitch—death. I managed to babble Luis's name. I tried to move but panic anchored me. The SUV swung wide with difficulty and missed him. Vadier sprang forward. "You fucking crazy cunt," a male voice shouted. I closed my eyes. Vadier wasn't there. Slow motion passed on to fast forward. I saw them huddled together in the puddle-filled gutter. The bus went by, blowing a fanfare with its horn. In those few seconds, my imagination ran free with the most irrational thoughts I've ever had in my life. Like a mediocre actor in front of a tough audience, I replayed the scene over and over again: We decided to cross. I looked both ways to make sure it was clear. There were no cars coming. I took a step forward, and then disaster struck. *Rewind*: We decided to cross. I looked both ways to make sure it was clear. No one was coming. I should have expected it. I should have known that he wasn't OK. I should have taken his hand and let him know that, despite feeling tortured, he could count on me. I could have let him know that he wasn't alone. The distant outline of two figures screaming at each other and fighting in the gutter brought me back to the world; however, I couldn't move. I reproached myself for my immobility, for standing there with my hands in my pockets, for my paralyzing cowardice. Luis punched Vadier in the face; blood spurted from his nose. Vadier kneed him in the stomach, knocking the wind out of him. The old people on the tour bus slowly emerged from their luxury coach, spectating the brawl. "Enough!" I shouted. *Rewind*: We decided to cross. I looked both ways to make sure it was clear. No one was coming. A bus appeared from one direction, an SUV from the other. "Move, stupid," Vadier shouted. Before the SUV passed by, Vadier managed to grab him by the neck and throw him to the curb. I had the impression that, as they flew across the road, the SUV grazed their ankles. There were two pairs of shoes in the air, dancing in full party mode. All of a sudden, Luis calmed down. He raised a fist. I managed to move my knees. My kneecap made a sound like a walnut being cracked. I had no breath, no blood, no strength, no words. I was like a crumpled rag doll. He looked right at me. The crowd muttered the usual comments. Vadier, wiping his lip, remained on the puddle-filled ground. Luis let him go and disappeared down a small street.

"Luis was on medication for a while. He came back from Europe a very different person. He wasn't the same. He was bitter, furious, angry at everything. And the best thing Señora Aurora could come up with was to force him to repeat the last year of high school. Armando was out of the country. Luis became withdrawn, unfriendly. He would only talk to Titina. She was the only one capable of reaching him, of speaking to him without getting him worked up. Then, gradually, things went back to normal. He went back to being his same old self, the same charming guy." I finished my hot chocolate. I was still thirsty and asked for a Coke. "Titina has a theory," Vadier said. I didn't follow him. I had the feeling I'd lost the thread of the conversation. "A theory about what?" I asked, confused. "About Luis, about his sudden change," he made a long pause. "You!" he said. "Titina thinks that Luis went back to being a cool guy the day he met you; the day he reluctantly allowed Señora Aurora to enroll him in the preparatory course. Titi and I both believe that the best thing that could ever have happened to him was meeting you. I swear, four months ago he was a miserable fucking wretch. Three months ago he was doing stupid things like pinching tires, spitting on pizzas, and scratching the paint on cars with that dickhead, Pelolindo. But when you appeared, everything changed. Titina believes that Luis is really hooked on you, and she knows him pretty well. Let me tell you something, Eugenia: Luis came back to Venezuela in mid-December. On New Year's Day he told Titi some crazy stuff. He told her that he was going to pull off some amazing feat, that he had to meet up with Samuel Lauro to organize God knows what kind of nonsense. Luis arranged the meeting with Samuel in early January. They arranged to meet during Carnival or Easter"— Vadier asked for another coffee —"Titina was convinced that if Luis met up with Samuel, he'd get into trouble, that something really bad would happen. But then, all of a sudden, you two met, and things changed. So don't think that Titi's angry with you; quite the opposite. All of us who know Luis well know that you're the only reason he's gone back to being relatively normal. Only you can help him. The rest of us are simply bystanders."

LAST NIGHT

1

Music>Artist>Maná>*Love Is a Battle* (13 songs)>"Your Divine Light." The road wound around sharp curves, through peaks named after animals. The cold air went up my nose. My throat hurt. The guitar affected me deeply. Guitars always get to me. "No kidding, what cheesy shit!" Luis said from the back of the car. "Shut your mouth! It's great. It's awesome. Juan Luis Guerra is the bomb," Vadier replied. The tension of Apartaderos had disappeared. "I refuse to listen to a merengue singer who's become a Christian evangelist. Much less singing a duet with those jerks from Maná. I can't stand that group of tree huggers." The trivial conversation took the pressure off things. At the same time, it created a taboo: nothing had happened in Apartaderos. None of us mentioned what had occurred on the road. The harsh images from that town seemed to have been deposited in an alternate reality. "If that dickhead, Bono, plants a tree and holds a concert in some godforsaken country in Africa, then he's a great guy. But if Fher, the lead singer from Maná, who's

Mexican and not Irish does it, then he's a pretentious snob who deserves to be ridiculed," Vadier complained. "Fuck, Vadier, you can't compare Maná to U2. That's blasphemy." "I think Maná are heaps better. Besides, I don't like Bono. Now there's a phony-ass environmentalist for you." Hysterical laughter. Luis was slumped in the back of the car, badly shaven, with pimples and dark circles under his eyes. The fear had disappeared from his eyes, and he seemed to have calmed down. "Do you remember *Vampi*?" he asked. "Why the fuck would we remember *Vampi*? That shit was on sometime in the early nineties. We would've been about three or four years old. Are you saying you watched it? You really are full of shit." "What the fuck is *Vampi*?" I asked. "A soap opera about a bunch of vampires who invade a small town. There are a few old episodes on YouTube," Luis said. He began to laugh again. "No. I was just imagining that if 'Sunday Bloody Sunday' had been the theme song to *Vampi*, it would've been totally wicked." Vadier shared in his hilarity. The entire way, they dreamed up absurd situations between Maná and U2: duets between Bono and Fher on MTV; Alex González and Larry Mullen exchanging drumsticks; Bono draped in a Mexican flag and Fher in an Irish one. One of them would say one thing, and the other would burst into hysterics. "Can you imagine Bono singing 'Rayando el sol'?" Vadier imitated the lead singer from U2: "'Scratching the sun...Oh, eh, oh. Desperation.' Fuck, you'd just say it as a joke, but The Edge would really rock the intro to Maná's 'Let me in.'" "You two are talking crap," I said, bored. I didn't understand anything. I didn't know who was who. My mind was occupied with recent memories, with Alfonso's letter and the image of Luis smashed to pieces. "This song is over the

of kindness with suspicion. I don't know whether Luis told his friends that he banged me, screwed me, or—to borrow a vulgar expression from the Maestro—that he fucked me till he shot his load out my ears. I loved Luis. I've never done, nor will I ever do, with anyone else what I did with Luis, not like that. In Mérida, I slept with another guy for the first time. My intimacy with Jorge had been a sham. I would just lie there and think about other things while he humped me like a dog in heat. Any stupid thought would be more interesting: exams, pending obligations, Eugenia's complaints, episodes of *Lost*. There were many times on hot, sultry afternoons in some hotel when I substituted Jorge's face with the faces of others: Leonardo DiCaprio, Juanes, Leopoldo López (a nobody mayor who seemed cute to me), and various others. With Luis it was different. When he expertly entered me, it felt as though a bolt of lightning shot through me. The weight of his body on mine made one of my lungs collapse. All our forms took on the effect of being doubled: four feet, twenty fingers, four knees, two navels, two noses. He put his index finger in my mouth and caressed my palate. His long fingernails scraped the insides of my cheeks. My belly felt disproportionately hot. For a moment, I thought my insides were made of butter. Poor Jorge! I know I've made him out to be clumsy and incompetent. To be honest, little Jorge needed to take his time. He found it difficult to enter me. He'd get lost, and he'd hurt me with his clumsy fingers. Without really know-ing why, my body just got used to remaining dry and unaroused. I don't want to relate details about what we did. Intimate confessions make me uncomfortable. They make me feel emo, foolish, like some maid in a soap opera who

of his own worthlessness: he was just like Alfonso. That thought made me feel like gagging and like I was getting a bout of diarrhea. To kill time, I decided to go through the dumpster that my backpack had turned into: inside were candy wrappers, empty bags of Doritos, old receipts, makeup, Alfonso's letter. At the bottom, shoved in between some aluminum foil that contained the remnants of a cheese pizza, I found Laurent's passport. It was filled with immigration stamps: Argentina, Bolivia, Peru, Jamaica. For the sake of my mental health, I shoved it back into the bag. I didn't want to think about the ghost of my grandfather. I continued rummaging through the backpack and found a jar of cream that I had once stolen from Natalia: Nivea Body Lotion with Ginkgo and Vitamin E. The walk in the sun had soaked my back, so I had another shower. I took my time, and I smeared myself with the lotion. When I came out of the bathroom, I found Luis sitting on the edge of the bed. I was afraid that he would launch into one of his defeatist monologues again. I didn't want to see him unhappy and, even less so, violent. He studied me with curiosity. Two white towels loosely covered me: one wrapped around my head and the other, like a housecoat, wrapped around my body. "I want to see you naked," he said frankly. He had a calm smile on his face. There was no sign of sadness in his eyes. His request impressed me. I didn't reply. "It's our last night together, isn't it? I told you that it would be special. You're the most beautiful piece of ass I've ever seen, Eugenia." The towel, like the panties in a common refrain, fell to the ground. I walked toward the bed and sat down by his side. I remembered something Natalia had said to me on the phone the day before I left: "Bitch, you need to

parking lot." "Fuck," I said, worried for him. Liquor stores, groceries, supermarkets, kiosks, all were closed. Luis hiked to a nearby gas station and bought two bags of ice. When he opened the door to the room he had a bottle of Blue Label in his hands. "It's the second last bottle," he said. "I couldn't get any wine. We'll have to celebrate with whisky." While Luis was taking a shower, I poured two shots. I went out onto the balcony and saw Vadier running around the Fiorino in circles like a whack job. He was lifting his knees to his chest as though he were performing exercises in a pre-military academy. The sound of running water suddenly stopped. The balcony was only ten feet from the bathroom—I'm bad at calculating distances; it could even have been three, four, or five feet. Luis emerged from the shower naked and stood in front of me. I suffered an imaginary fainting fit. I was breathing awkwardly. In my thirty years, I can say that I know what a man's body is like. I've seen at least a dozen guys naked from that distance. Luis was the only one capable of inspiring thoughts of beauty. The rest—some hairy, others smooth—paraded their masculinity exclusively through their tool, through their slimy manhood. For his part, Luis came together in one harmonious package, of skin and eyes, of hair and biceps, of sex and face. He walked slowly over to the bed. He took a sip of whisky. He wasn't fully erect. Halfway to getting hard, he seemed to waver between getting it up or letting it go down. Objectively speaking, dicks are ugly, grotesque you could even say. The misfortune of being in love prompts me to say that Luis's was particularly beautiful and impressive; which, by the way, I still don't refute. Without a doubt, the person who came off badly as a result of my little

mouth was amusing itself with his nipple. The bottle of whisky, half full or half empty, was beside him. "Explain your theory of coincidence to me. What's it about?" I kissed his neck, his lips, his right eye. "I believe that God exists, but that he's powerless. He can't do everything. God's cool, and he has good ideas, but human beings complicate everything too much. And then sometimes things happen in life that coincide with God's plan, and that's what I call coincidence." "Huh?" I said, lifting my face. "I didn't understand a thing. You've lost me." "It's like that awful song by that Christian evangelist." "Which Christian evangelist?" "That horrible song that Juan Luis Guerra sings with Maná, what we were listening to in the car. I thought he said: 'divine coincidence.' If God is good, then he must think it's kind of cool that we're together here today. If he doesn't care less about what we've done, then God's a dumb jerk." "You sound just like the priests at school." "Priests are often right. The problem is they don't know how to say things. A guy who has to hide from the world that on a hot, sultry morning he feels like sucking tits, or jerking off, must have a skewed vision of reality." He moved down to my chest, bit my nipples, continued further down, circling around my navel before dipping his tongue into it. "Luis"— I took advantage of the circumstances, the feeling of trust —"what happened on the road? What the fuck was all that? Why?" He lifted his gaze to meet mine. His eyes went from lively ochre to melancholy russet—like the names they give colored pencils. I told him not to fear me, that I would never abandon him. I was telling him the truth. I know that people often say stupid things like this and then, after swearing on their mother's life, break up two weeks later. But at that moment, I tried to be sincere. Venezuelan mothers are apt to make use of the fable of the cliff when scolding their children: kids with weak characters tend to imitate their more daring friends, sometimes with disastrous consequences. That's when the mother poses her philosophical question: if your friend jumped off a cliff, would you follow him too? Goddammit, sure I would! What's the problem with that? I said to myself. If Luis Tévez had thrown himself off a cliff, I would have gone after him. "Sometimes I get scared," he said. "What scares you?" "I don't know, everything. I can't explain it. It's a kind of fear and desperation. I don't know what else to tell you." "You scared the shit out of me"— I gave him a loving smack across the head —"I thought you'd been smashed to pieces." He kissed me, and shrugged his shoulders. "I'm sorry. I won't hurt you ever again. What'll we do when we get back to Caracas?" he asked me. "Will you go back with Jorge?" "It's true, we never broke up officially, but don't worry, Jorge doesn't exist; he's just a phantom." He sat down on the bed and had a shot of whisky. "Are we a couple, Eugenia Blanc? How cool! I've never had a serious girlfriend before. Well, OK, I did have one but she doesn't count." "I'd hate to be an irritating girlfriend, a zelophobe, someone corny. I don't want us to get on each other's nerves." "It's inevitable, Princess. It's a human trait. Human beings are condemned to captivating one another and then getting on each other's nerves two days later"— he paused —"although God would never allow me to get annoyed with you," he concluded. "Dammit, enough already about God. You're making me nervous. You make me feel as though I've just sucked Father Peñaloza's cock." "Trust me, the old guy wouldn't mind." "Ugh, dis-

of shit and we stop seeing each other after July. I don't know what's going to happen to us. But the year I turn thirty, I want to remember this moment and celebrate it with you, getting drunk on whisky. How does that sound?" "It sounds great. I'll be there, whatever happens. Where'll we meet—in Paris?" "I don't know, in whatever part of the world. Now it's your turn to make a stupid promise," I said, imagining that he would take his time, that he would expound some sort of complex, erudite idea, something that would be difficult for me to understand. He replied immediately. I felt joy and terror: "I'm going to marry you, Eugenia." "Fuck!" I replied. I wasn't expecting that. "What's wrong? Don't you want to?" "Yeah, sure I do. I've got no problem with it." "But?" he asked, speeding up his thrusts, increasing his pace as he pounded into me. "I think marriage is bullshit. I just see it as a sham." "Ours will be different. I agree with you, I don't know why people get married." "For the same reason we're gonna do it, because we're dumb," I managed to get out between inescapable moans, with my air passages blocked. "I would never ask you to get married in a church or a registry office. There'd be no fun in that. Nor would I demand that we brush our teeth in the same basin or that you had to take a piss while I shaved. The kind of marriage I'm offering would take place on our terms, informally, illegally perhaps, but definitely special. A compromise between you and me. How does that sound?" He slowed down his thrusts, pulled me toward him, and stopped moving from his waist; the movement occurred internally. "OK, great, let's get married right away," I said, just to say something. "Cool," he replied. Then he performed an unexpected stunt. He lifted me up and let me fall back onto the bed.

Supporting his body with one hand on my shoulder, he shot his load over me after ten rough and brutal strokes. My eyes rolled back into my head. My legs went weak. I moaned with pleasure. I didn't climax, but without question I was floating. He got up anxiously and put on his pants and shoes. "What's wrong?" I asked him, after coming back down to earth. "Get dressed," he said. "Put something on. I'll go and get Vadier." "Vadier? Why do you want to—" He interrupted me: "Well, clearly someone has to do it: Vadier will marry us."

2

Vadier ordered us to kneel down. His face was without form. He looked like a beggar. He was drooling and laughing to himself. He asked us to take each other by the hand and face one another. Then he emptied a bottle of whisky over us: "I, representing Old Johnnie Walker, unite you in unholy matrimony, hardcore, Marlboro, tits, bim-bam-boom, ass, Spiderman, dick, Michael Jackson. Amen." Then he grabbed a bag of Cheetos and stomped on it: "Mazel Tov," he shouted, or something like that. "You may now make out with each other," he said with solemnity. I felt like Fiona, Shrek's bride. That could have been the final chapter, the happy finale. But things never work out like that. I wish the credits had started to roll at that moment. Vadier jumped onto the bed and began to spin like a top. Luis walked over to the little table where my iPod was. "All that's left for us to do now is dance, Princess. Will you permit me the honor?" "Of course," I said, laughing. My face reeked of whisky. I thought that he would play "Losing My Religion." Having heard it so many times and commented on it, I'd eventually learned its name. I don't know how that song ended up on my playlist. Luis seemed awkward. It took him some time to figure out the buttons. "I don't have Bob Dylan on my iPod, Luis. You won't find 'Visions of Johanna.'" He ignored my sarcasm. "Here it is," he said. "I told you that in this type of a relationship one has to make sacrifices."

Goddammit! I said to myself. Low blow. He almost made me cry. I hate crying. I never cry. I didn't cry that time either, but I must admit that my eyes welled up: the acoustic guitar dealt me at least four blows. He came over to me and took me into his arms. At first we improvised a waltz, although in truth, I don't really know how to waltz. "One day, calmness comes over me/My Peter Pan rouses today/There's little left to do here/I feel like I'm somewhere else/Somewhere alone at home/It'll be your skin that's to blame (0:30)." "Reggaeton," he said. Then we grinded. He took me by the waist and rubbed himself up and down against me to the slow rhythm of El Canto del Loco. "It must be because I've grown older/That something new has pressed this button/For Peter to leave/And maybe now I'll live much better/More at ease and at peace inside myself/May Tinkerbell take care of you and watch over you (0:52)." "Tango," he said. He straightened his spine, stretched out his right arm, put his hand on my hip, and led me in a sloppy march around the room. When we reached the bathroom door, we switched positions. He stretched out his other arm, put his leg behind my knee, and gave me a little push. Vadier began jumping up and down on top of the bed. And the Locos sang on: "At times you shout from the heavens/Wanting to destroy all my calm/Coming after me like thunder/To give me that bolt of blue lightning./Now you shout to me from the heavens/But you encounter my soul/Don't try anything with me/It seems that love calms me down…it calms me down (1:17)." "Ballet," he said. My laugh was horrible. It emerged deep from within my diaphragm, making a cackling sound. He put his feet together; spread them apart; he stood on tiptoes; he put his hands on his head and began spinning like a top. Beyond a doubt, happiness lies in stupidity. We often underestimate the significance of being absurd. I have to admit that watching Luis doing ballet while Vadier jumped up and down on that motel bed is one of the best things that has ever happened to me. It wasn't just a bit of ordinary fun. It wasn't just being silly. Nothing has given me so much peace as those acts of intimacy. Somehow, letting go and being silly is a form of liberation. Vadier took out a knife from his bag and tore open a pillow. "If you take away my child-hood/Take the part I no longer need/If you leave, I will live with the peace that I need/And that I've yearned for (1:40)." Our dance during the next verse was normal. We didn't improvise any Hungarian marches or traditional Dominican merengues. Vadier, who had transformed into someone resembling the superhero Hellboy, ran around the room tossing feathers in the air and shouting phrases in English. "But one fine day/It seemed he wanted to stay here with me/There was no way to get rid of him/If Peter doesn't want to leave/The loneliness will want to live on in me/Life goes through its phases, its phases (2:05)." After that verse a ukulele came on. Then the drums and the salsa. Luis was a klutz, a rotten dancer. He mimicked the dance steps awkwardly. During one chorus we improvised a paso doble. Luis placed a finger on my head and then started running around me in circles, slapping his knee with his free hand. Vadier got

arrived at El Rosal. Beneath the highway overpass in Las Mercedes, two thugs asked me for money, making out they were armed. I have never felt such honest contempt toward anyone as I did for those two pieces of shit. I asked them politely to get lost. I told them that they'd end up drowned in the Guaire River and that their bodies would become mincemeat for stray dogs and scavengers if they didn't clear off in less than ten seconds. For some unknown reason they took fright. They stared at me as if I were crazy. Natalia messaged me that the funeral would be held in the East Cemetery.

We left Vadier at Querales's place. Rafa, whom I only knew by sight, was a grotesque, legendary figure who had barely scraped through primary school. Vadier and Querales gave each other a manly hug, belched, and spat out various profanities. Querales entered his house, leaving the front door open. Vadier approached the Fiorino and kissed Luis's cheek. "Don't do anything stupid, man, stay calm. See you in Caracas." He showed no signs of a hangover, there was no stench of alcohol about him. There was no evidence of the plumed priest he had transformed into the night before. "Your Majesty," he said, looking me in the eye and bowing low, "take care." He walked away from the car and left. Then the Fiorino made a U-turn. Before he entered Querales's house, Vadier called out with great fanfare: "Tévez! Téeeveeez!" Luis put on the brakes. During the second cry, Vadier beat his chest three times with his left fist while holding a bottle of Blue Label in his right hand. Then he disappeared behind the door. Luis spat out a laugh: ha, ha, ha. "What happened?" I asked. "What was all that about?" "He's saying goodbye like Francesco Quinn in

Platoon." "Like who?" "Haven't you ever seen *Platoon*?" "No," I answered honestly. "Do you know who Charlie Sheen is?" "Isn't he the guy in *Two and a Half Men*?" He revved up the engine. He took my hand and said, "Fuck, Princess, your ignorance is encyclopedic."

The lid of the coffin was closed. "Luis turned to shit," Vadier would say to me later. The Maestro was devastated. Floyd sat in front of the coffin, stroking the lid with one hand. Señora Aurora didn't attend the funeral. Someone told me that she'd been sedated in some clinic. The school sent wreaths with prefabricated messages. Natalia, Claudia Gutiérrez, and various other jerks howled in frenzy, as if in deep mourning. Jorge accompanied me in silence. He didn't say anything. He just stood by my side, looking at me with the face of a sad puppy dog. Like Natalia, he was surprised by my familiarity with all those weirdos: Mel Camacho, Claire, José Miguel, and, in particular, Titina. He didn't accuse me of anything, but he did ask some questions out of turn. I broke up with Jorge during the funeral. It has to be one of the lamest ways to put an end to a relationship. I was quite rough on him. I said things to him I shouldn't have. My words were barbed, venomous. Vadier was the last one to arrive. He was shaved. Clean. With his shirt tucked in. At first I didn't recognize him. "Your Majesty," he said to me in a low voice. All my repressed feelings—my mute sadness, my stifled grief, my anger, my questions—were released from their moorings. I hugged him with unrestrained, overdone desperation. My hug with Vadier—I found out later—was the most talked about thing during recess at school in the following weeks. I didn't want to let go of him. He was the closest thing I had to Luis, the most alike, the most intimate, what we shared in common. When I threw my arms around his neck, my legs gave way beneath me. Clinging to his shoulders for support, my feet almost dragging along the ground, I somehow managed to sit down. In the seats behind us, a few idiots from Class B were making jokes. After a long and intense silence, Vadier gave me the family's version of what happened: Luis tripped and fell through the window. One of the idiots from Class B let out a huge laugh. Realizing the inappropriateness of her behavior, she immediately covered her mouth. "What do you believe?" I asked him. "What do you think happened?" "I don't know. The story about him falling over from being intoxicated is a typical Tévez tale. Besides, Luis left a note." The noise from the seat behind continued. I couldn't help myself. At the next giggle, I turned around: "Shut the fuck up, you stupid bitches! We're at a funeral. Go and watch a porno. Go and suck someone's dick or laugh at all your stupidities somewhere else. This shit here's a cemetery. Show some fucking respect." The three dumbasses stared at me in disgust, and then left. Later on, someone told me that I'd committed social suicide with that outburst. I became public enemy number one in my class at school. "Amen," Vadier said. "What did the note say?" I asked, ignoring the interruption. "No one knows. It was addressed personally." "Who was it addressed to?" Vadier took my hand. "Luis just left a note for Floyd."

On the road back I slept for several hours. We listened to Dylan. Only Dylan. "Visions of Johanna" played at least twelve times. My body hurt, my jaw ached, my buttocks burned, and my thighs trembled. After our wedding celebration with Johnnie Walker, we had to carry Vadier to the

Fiorino. The hotel room was a mess. Goose feathers—or duck or stone-curlew or condor or synthetic—were strewn all over the room. That night we fucked about nine times. Around six in the morning, Luis said that he couldn't do it anymore, that he had nothing left inside him. Mérida was a debauchery, an excess. I woke up when we arrived in Victoria. Luis was humming along to Dylan's songs, shaking his head. I stared at him with a stupid expression on my face, with my mouth open, studying him, scrutinizing his pores. "I love you," I blurted out suddenly. How creepy! I said to myself. I had never said anything like that before. I didn't even mean to say it. It just came out. I couldn't avoid it. Nor did I try to stop myself. My immune system didn't put up any resistance. He said nothing. He took my left hand and kissed my knuckles.

When we arrived in Caracas, we parked outside Floyd's place. I was ticked off. All I wanted to do was dive into my bed and sleep for the next thirty-six hours. Luis said that after dropping by Floyd's, he had to leave the Fiorino in the parking lot at the factory. We'd go back to our own places by cab. "How annoying having to go to Floyd's! Can't you go tomorrow?" "No. It has to be now." Floyd took ages coming down. I stayed in the Fiorino. Luis got out of the car and spoke with Floyd in the entrance to the apartment building. I was distracted. I paid no attention to them. My belly ached. I thought that if I were to accidentally scratch it, instead of blood, semen would come out. Suddenly, Luis made a gesture at me. Floyd acknowledged him. He seemed to be saying, "Her, take a good look at her." Floyd asked him something with a confused gesture. I couldn't work out what Luis explained to him. Floyd kept staring at me with his sick animal eyes. Luis gave him two of the three cameras that he'd brought along on the trip—the biggest ones. Floyd stood there like a tree stump as the Fiorino pulled away. "Now, Princess," Luis said, "off to the factory."

A week after Luis's death, Eugenia talked to me. She told me that my dad had called the house and that he wanted to tell me something important. Eugenia gave him permission to come over and see me at our apartment. When Alfonso came to our place, my mom went out. She invented a pressing engagement. "Hi, Eugenia," said the phony-assed poseur. I greeted him with false courtesy. He made a few trivial comments that didn't interest me. I quickly got tired of him. I wanted him to leave. According to Eugenia, he wanted to tell me something important. But after fifteen minutes had gone by, he still hadn't said anything of note. He just babbled a few cheesy phrases about the family and gave me a box of chocolates. "What do you want, Alfonso? Why have you come here?" I was annoyed. I decided to confront him. He sat down on a kitchen stool. "I know that you were in Altamira. How was it? Did you like my surprise?" "To be honest, no, I didn't. Although I should've expected it from you. It's typical of you to do something like that." What did he expect—that I'd run over to him and give him a hug, tell him I forgive him, tell him I smell gas every morning just to remember him? Give me time, Alfonso, don't pressure me, don't push me, I said to myself. "I came to give you some forms," he said, getting up and taking out a few papers from a manila folder. "They're for the scholarship from the Ayacucho Founda-tion. Read over the material, see if you're interested, and let me know your decision. Do you know what you want to study?" "No. Not really." "What do you like?" "Nothing." "I also brought you a few brochures with university offers in Europe: Madrid, London, Paris. Take your time and read them. You'll find more information on the internet." I didn't even thank him. I made a rude show of indifference and let him talk alone. He just stood there. He looked like a rag doll, like a dummy, like one of those plastic fishes that hang on the walls in bars, shaking their heads and singing popular songs. In that conversation, I managed to figure out what I felt for my dad: total indifference. The smell of gasoline was too strong.

The Fiorino broke down two blocks from the factory. A cloud of gray smoke covered the windshield. Luis got nervous. "Goddammit!" I said, opening the hood. "This piece of shit has overheated." "What?" he asked. "It's overheated," I said again. "What do you have to do?" "I don't know. I think we have to put some water into something called a radiator." "And where do we find that?" "I have no idea, I think it's this thing here," I said, pointing to the box that Garay had left the pliers on. "Do we have any water?" I asked. He shook his head. "How much farther to the factory?" "About two blocks." I decided to check in the back of the car. I had a feeling that I'd seen Vadier with a bottle of mineral water at one point. "Anything?" he asked, terrified. "Nothing." "Fuck, what'll we do now? I can't leave the Fiorino here. Garay would get mad, and it wouldn't be right. Garay's a friend." A gleam from the corner in the back of the car caught my eye. It was the last bottle of Blue Label. "Let's put some whisky in this piece of shit," I said with confidence. "What?" "There are only two blocks to go.

What's the worst that could happen?" "Cool!" I grabbed the bottle. The smoke from the motor continued forming dirty clouds. "Where's the thing we have to fill up?" Luis asked. I took off the boiling cap and rested the tip of the bottle on the lip of the radiator. "Wait, wait," he said to me. He ran to his seat, and came back with a digital camera. "OK, go on." I poured in the whisky. I emptied the bottle between several clicks. Then, the Fiorino fired up. It made a very strange noise, but we managed to get it to the parking lot. "Let Garay fix this mess!" When Luis turned off the motor, I heard the final verses of "Visions of Johanna" for the last time. We tossed the last bottle of Blue Label into a yellow trash can.

I cut myself off from Jorge and Natalia. Between April and July, school turned into a torture chamber. I didn't go back to the preparatory course or to Doctor Fragachán's useless therapy sessions. In the afternoons, I met up with Titina in a café to talk about trivial stuff. We bumped into each other a few times at the Tecniciencias Bookstore in the San Ignacio mall, and after that we carried on a casual, light-hearted, but sadly brief friendship. We seldom spoke of Luis. We rented movies from Blockbuster and met up with Vadier to waste time—Vadier said that in the end, life was nothing more than a permanent waste of time. They were heavy days, endlessly muggy. The group of misfits from San Carlos got together at a party at Nairobi's house. Everyone was there, including the Patriot, whom I'd forgotten about. He handed us a leaflet that stated he was a student representative of I don't know which university. I think it was the Andrés Bello Catholic University. Mel, for his part, told us that he planned to set up a company called

El Astillero Cyber-Café, about which he didn't want to give any details. We were all drunk before midnight. There was no atmosphere. There was no music. There were no jokes or *peomas*. Luis's absence made everything strange. Each person clung to his own melancholy. Vadier, Titina, and I snuck out onto the balcony. "Did you see today's paper?" Vadier asked, somewhat groggy. He was smoking a blue joint that Mel had bought off some Bulgarians. "I never read the paper," Titina said. "Didn't you see the internet?" "The internet's only good for porno," she replied. "What happened?" "Some guy went over to the National Parliament this morning and blew himself up." Titina let out a laugh. "What?" "Nothing happened. The dude just killed himself. He got all nervous and exploded the device before entering the floor. The MPs, more shit scared than a little kid's diaper, were giving press conferences like crazy, trampling over one another to tell their story to anyone who'd listen. I saw it on the news about three hours ago. It looks like Samuel Lauro's headed for prison." Silence. Grimaces. Staring at the bottom of our glasses. "Do you think Luis really wanted to do something as stupid as that?" Titina asked. "I don't know. I have no idea. Maybe." "What did Luis and Samuel talk about in Mérida?" I asked curiously. Luis never told me what happened at that meeting. Vadier and Titina looked at one another knowingly. "Nothing," Vadier replied. "They never met up. Luis came with me to Querales's house. Do you remember? Querales wasn't at home. We talked to his sister, who's a total nut job. Then Luis left, because he said he had to meet up with Lauro. I was really annoyed. So I ended up following him. He walked to some place where Samuel was supposedly working. The jerk was fixing a photocopier and watching a Beyoncé concert on TV. Luis just stood there staring at him for a while. In the end, he didn't go in, Eugenia. He stuck his head in, asked the price of a printer cartridge, and left. He walked around the city and then went to bang you." We stayed up to dawn talking shit. Nairobi tried to lighten the reunion by proposing drunken party games: Pass the Orange, Never Have I Ever, and Spin the Bottle. Around five thirty in the morning, I was reamed out by the Patriot: "Eugenia, you have to take part in our movement. Your country needs you. We're the new generation. You and I have to fight." I looked him up and down and laughed in his face: "Fight? No, you dumbass. Hulk Hogan fought." I never did know who the hell Hulk Hogan was.

We walked hand in hand to Avenida Rómulo Gallegos. We kissed on every corner without shame. Luis called one of his cabdriver friends. He had four or five private numbers on his cell phone. The cab took half an hour to arrive. Half an hour of kisses, of tongue, of silly words, of daffy caresses. We spent the ride home touching and fondling each other. The cabdriver was meant to drop me off first and then take Luis to his building. We arrived quickly. The city was deserted. There was no traffic. I didn't want to get out of the car. I found it hard to open the door. I said goodbye with a kiss on the lips. "Princess," he said as I was getting out, "come here." He looked uneasy. He wanted to tell me something but he seemed to be tongue-tied. "About the name 'Princess'...I told you that it was Titina and Nairobi who...well...the truth is...it wasn't them...I... this...I don't know...to me...it was..." "I get it, Luis. It's very sweet. Bye, see you Monday." I gave him a simple kiss, and I got out of the cab. "Eugenia," he cried out with that inevitable look of melancholy in his eyes, "don't forget your promise. I've fulfilled mine." He rolled up the window. We never saw one another again.

2

Titina Barca's real name was Cristina Bárcenas. Her nickname dates back to primary school. Her grandmother had a cat called Titina, and she fell in love with that name when she was a little girl. I found out her real identity when I went to see her at the Loira Clinic. She was supposed to be in room 1404. I had to climb fourteen floors, because the elevators weren't working. Titina's name wasn't pasted on any of the doors. I asked some of the nurses, and none of them knew what to tell me. According to them, she wasn't there. As I was walking back down the stairs, on the twelfth floor I came across José Miguel, who was out of breath. I told him what had happened to me, and he just laughed. "Jeez, Eugenia. Who the fuck would be called Titina? No one's called Titina. Titi's called Cristina. Cristina Bárcenas."

Cancer. Damned cancer. It returned with a vengeance, and it sucked her life away in less than three months. A few days before my graduation, I got the news: Titina was shooting penalties, as Vadier would say. She didn't have much time left. Natalia was still mad at me from Easter. Over the past few months she had gotten close with Claudia Gutiérrez and, what's worse, she told Jorge a load of bull about me. She told him secrets and details he didn't need to know. Jorge's friends also began to treat me with contempt. I graduated from high school alone, without my old friends, without any of my peers, and with the reputation of being a slut. Alfonso showed up at the auditorium in a yellow jacket and a shiny gold necklace. I was very embarrassed. However, I greeted him with affection. His effort to love me gradually stopped seeming phony to me. I decided to take him at his word. "I need your help, Alfonso. Get me out of here," I muttered under my breath, posing for the official photo. For the most part, the ceremony was homage to melodrama. The speech by our valedictorian, Gonzalo, was regrettable. Professor Mariana, the head teacher, read out something that no one understood and then ended with the hackneyed lines of a poem addressed to a wayfarer: the path, the path that doesn't exist, and the fucker who makes his own path by walking. The ceremony was an utter farce. Jorge looked like a real Ken doll, with his gray suit and his sharp fringe. I knew that he had a girlfriend. He'd hooked up with that private-school bimbo, the one he danced reggaeton with one unforgettable night, a few months back. "Eugenia Blanc," the MC called out on the microphone. I stood up. Out of the corner of my eye, I could see that Natalia wasn't applauding. Her indifference hurt me. Deep down I valued her friendship. She whispered something to Claudia Gutiérrez and giggled theatrically. I walked up to the podium alone, in silence. The applause that accompanied me was a gesture of courtesy on the part of some of those present. The buzz of gossip made my ears prickle. I felt like turning around and telling each person there to go eat a plate of shit. After shaking the hands of a row of obnoxious teachers and being handed my diploma by the priest, I heard someone yell out: "YOUR MAJESTY!" Followed by whistles, noisemakers, curses, "Hell, yeahs," and trumpet sounds made by mouth. "Eugeniaaaaaa!

excruciating and indescribable. In those days of chemotherapy, nausea, and tremors, she told me many things. She told me about her family, about her first two boyfriends, about her unclassifiable relationship with Luis. "Nairobi won't come over to my place again," she told me one afternoon when she was feeling terrible. I said nothing. "I always thought of her as my best friend. Friendship is a mirror, Eugenia. At the moment of truth, the majority of people flee," she said between laughter and burping up gas. "What happened?" "Nothing. She came over yesterday, saw me, and began to cry. Am I that horrible to look at?" "Do you want the truth?" I asked prudently. "Please." "OK, here goes: yes, Titi, you look atrocious." "Goddammit!" "I think it's normal for people to get a shock when they see you. You look like shit." She weighed eighty pounds, she had gray hair—the little that was left—and her face was covered in spots. She'd suffered an allergic reaction to one of her medications. "All the same, it makes me mad, goddammit!" she said. "We're supposed to be friends. She told me she couldn't bear seeing me like this, and then she took off like a bat out of hell. That struck me as cowardly. It's pure bullshit." "José Miguel came by this morning," I said to her. She smiled sweetly, without burping up any annoying gas. "That fatty is loyal. Did I tell you that José Miguel proposed to me, about a year ago?" "That clown?" "Yes, girl, it was hilarious. The guy could think of no better way to declare his love than in a Chinese restaurant." "Son of a bitch! How pathetic!" "He's cute. That little fatty's a really good person." "Fuck, but he's so ugly and crude." "Sure he's a clown, but he makes me feel good when he comes to visit. In the end, you can never be sure who'll stand by you and who'll kick your ass." A somewhat long silence ensued. "By the way, he brought me a poem." "A poem or a *peoma*?" I asked. "A hybrid, I think. It's over there. I'll get it." She tried to get up and experienced a pain in her chest. She began to breathe with difficulty. "Stay there, I'll get it." "Damned cancer. It hurts like hell!" she said with frustration. Then she recovered her usual voice. "It's over there, between the pages of a magazine." I grabbed the bit of paper. "Read it aloud. You'll laugh your ass off." I read slowly, almost spelling out every word: "I still see your face in the Chinese restaurant, in the fish tank filled with piranhas that gnaw on my heart / I still read your name in the Chinese restaurant, in the menu with little pictures while I'm dying of loneliness / I'm still looking for your eyes in the Chinese restaurant, and I eat them with chopsticks, waiting for your return to the world." "How sweet of the fatty!" I said. "It's the most beautiful *peoma* that anyone has ever written me." "Is it true that you once won an erotic poetry contest?" I asked, recalling old rumors. That award was part of her legend. "That was all just nonsense," she said. "I did win an award for a bit of stuff that I wrote. It was an erotic poetry contest organized by the School of Arts at the Andrés Bello Catholic University. Some fat guy with an Italian surname arranged it. The fact is, they opened up the contest, and several of us entered. Mel, who'd completed two years at Arts, told me that the fat Italian guy was a sleazebag and that all I had to do to win the prize was write 'tits' or 'ass' or 'pussy' in every way possible, so that's what I did. I wrote one thing called 'The Infinite Anus' and a few other things called 'The Murderous Tit,' 'The Bipolar Nipple,' and 'Ass Hairs on My Pillow.' I wrote pure crap, pure useless shit. Curiously, though, I was awarded first prize. The day of the

you promise me something?" "Yeah, tell me. What's the deal?" I looked at the television: Homer was telling Moe about a problem he had at work. Bart called the bar and made a joke that got lost in translation. "Listen, Eugenia," she said: "Live!" "OK, what do I have to promise?" "Just that: live. In spite of everything, being alive is great. You get caught up in a lot of bullshit, Eugenia. I'm asking you to live, dammit. I want you to promise me that shit." I kissed her icy forehead, and nodded my acceptance with a pained sob and a wayward tear. Then I took her hand and sat down to watch *The Simpsons*. We fell asleep right away. It was about ten o'clock in the evening. Much later, the nurse would write down in her notebook that Cristina Bárcenas died at 11:34 p.m. The fucking flatline noise, which I'd seen and heard in so many movies, didn't wake me up. In real life, it sounds so different.

3

My imaginary Luis also appeared at Maiquetía International Airport. I hadn't lost the strange feeling of being guarded by a presence that never lost sight of me. Vadier had come to see me off. Both Eugenia and Alfonso thought that he was my boyfriend, but neither of them said anything. Amid all the hubbub, the soldiers, the line to pay the departure tax, and the mountain of suitcases, I thought I saw Luis leaning against a barricade. When I looked more carefully, my gaze only encountered hordes of children and outraged mothers flashing angry looks. Eugenia said goodbye coldly. What little affection I have for this woman! I said to myself. She's completely invisible to me. I never knew her, she never knew me. She brought me into this world, and we simultaneously disowned one another. Alfonso began to cry. He hugged me, he sniffled on me, he drooled on me. "Bye, Dad, thanks," I said, forcing a smile. "Your Majesty," Vadier said when it came to his turn, "see you soon." I walked toward the customs gate. Before scanning my boarding pass, I spontaneously turned around: "Vadier!" I shouted. In his eyes I saw the same old complicity. I beat my fist twice against my chest. He raised his arms, seeking an explanation. "Nothing," I called back to him. It was so crowded. We could barely hear each other. "I wanted to say goodbye like Francesco Quinn in the final scene in *Platoon*." "Like who?" "Charlie Sheen!" I shouted. "Who the hell is that?"

The National Guard humiliated me. I had to go through a scanner, strip in front of a fat woman, sing a verse of the National Anthem to some dumbass, go down to the airport runway so they could recheck my luggage, and respond to the feral questions of a gorilla in heat. "Are you carrying any drugs, citizen?" Yeah, you motherfucker, I've got fifty pounds of heroin shoved up my ass and a stomach full of cocaine-filled condoms, I felt like shouting. "No, I'm not carrying anything," I said politely. The flight was delayed for three hours. The military police rechecked all the passengers before we entered the plane. A stinking fat guy, squashed into a filthy uniform, carried out the final interrogation. When I finally set foot on the plane, I swore that I would never go back to that shithole of a country. It was the only promise I kept.

some air, wandering through a park filled with decrepit old couples moving around with the aid of walkers. Pedro Pablo Lorena, who could that be? I wondered. I'd never heard the name before. Over the years, Luis Tévez had become a faded memory, just an occasional and sad presence in the affections of a young girl—and one that eventually got lost. I got used to living without thinking about Venezuela, to being French without actually being so, to being a perpetual foreigner, a kind of alien that had no place in any part of the world. I hate France. I can't stand the French. I've tried to live separate from others, to find a simple kind of formula that allows me to go through life without getting hurt. That strange afternoon—that April 14—dug up my memories of Luis. It also summoned up the memory of my only friend, Vadier. We hadn't seen each other for three years, but we both knew that the distance that separated us was unimportant. Spurred by the memory of Luis's death, I remembered my brother Daniel's pale face and the smell of mothballs from a room where a friend died of cancer. A vivid image sprang to mind: Vadier singing aloud songs I'd long since forgotten. Some kids rode past on bikes. One of them looked just like Luis. He had a mean expression on his face. He grabbed fistfuls of dirt and threw them at his friends while verbally abusing them. I remembered a song about Peter Pan—I hadn't heard it in years. I didn't even know who sang it. That's what Luis was like: a guy who never grew up. A fruity, gooey, hotchpotch of memories. What he might have become. Maybe something good. The imagined melody brought up a memory of a hotel room and, with it, the obligation of a promise. I had completely forgotten about that stupid promise. I suddenly felt very curious

get it. She said that she would be staying with me for two weeks only. In the beginning, I thought it would be the worst fortnight of my life. But by the end of it, she turned out to be pleasant company. Initial reproach gave way to reconciliation, to mutual recognition. We weren't mother and daughter; we were two different women sharing unhappy stories. Eugenia could be a nice person. Her greatest failure was motherhood. I showed her the city, we got drunk, and at one drinking session, we sought forgiveness for our common failures. One morning, while she was helping me clean my little hovel (the Polish girl had gone home to Warsaw on vacation), something unusual happened: "Eugenia, who is Luis Tévez?" The question caught me off guard. I stood there holding the vacuum cleaner without knowing what to say. "Why do you ask?" "A few months ago I found your old school notebooks," she said. "What?" "About two months ago, when I was moving house, I found your notebooks. I was going to throw them all out, but, unintentionally, I started reading the back pages. What you wrote is very you, Eugenia. Aside from all the profanities, I think you write very well. You talk about Jorge, about Natalia. I hope you don't mind that I read them, but it was the only way I could get to know you. You also talk about your dad and me. What you say is quite direct." We both fell silent. I looked like a statue holding a vacuum cleaner. "You mention a guy by the name of Luis Tévez a lot. It seems he was someone important to you. Who was he, a boyfriend?" I switched on the vacuum cleaner, pushed aside some furniture, and threw some old magazines into the trash. "No one, Eugenia. He was just a friend, a high school boyfriend." I was vacuuming in a daze. Eugenia mother went to her room. She opened her suitcase, took out a bag, inspected the contents, and handed it to me: inside it were my English, Psychology, Earth Sciences notebooks, etc.

There were two envelopes and a letter inside the package: *Hi, Eugenia. Vadier Hernández gave me your address. You probably don't remember me as Pedro. Back in those days, everyone called me Floyd. One time, I saw this film with Brad Pitt where he was smoking a Honey Bear bong. His character's name was Floyd. After that, like the scatterbrained teenager that I was, I decided to take it on as an alias. I'm writing on behalf of Luis. I had to make sure you got this package on this particular date. I specifically instructed the idiots at DHL to deliver it precisely on April 14, 2020, not a day earlier nor a day later. I've enclosed two sealed envelopes with this letter. Inside them, you'll find a few things that, according to my brother, belong to you. He told me that you would know exactly what you had to do on this date. I've kept an old promise that's been pending for many years and that, for a period of time—the time you were still living in Venezuela—proved quite tough for me. Sending this package to you on this day was the only thing left for me to do, something I owed to Luis. When he died, he left me all of his cameras and developing equipment—much to his crazy old lady's resentment. My dad, Armando Tévez, was executor of my brother's will. I'm a photographer now. I live in Miami, and I work for a men's fashion magazine. I got married, I got divorced, I have a two-year-old son, who fortunately looks like his mom, and nothing more. That just about sums up my life, which probably doesn't interest you. I suppose I should apologize for invading your privacy. I hope you're well, Eugenia. Pedro P. Lorena—or if you prefer, your brother-in-law, Floyd. (Luis told me in a letter that you guys got married. I didn't quite get him.)*

It started to rain. The envelopes were heavy. That afternoon I walked around the city, doing multiple laps around my memories. A friend from work rang and said that a few of the staff were meeting up to get drunk in some bar downtown. Claiming prior commitments, I turned down the invitation. Eugenia mother had left, never to return. She moved to Argentina and married a pizza chef. Alfonso, who grew wealthy on the back of Chavismo, fell into disgrace with the new government. I think they even put him in prison. We saw each other in Paris some years ago, before the fall of the military regime. I could finally forgive my dad. I learned to put up with the smell of gasoline. After all, mediocrity doesn't rule out feeling affection for someone. A thunderclap announced a storm. Rain clouds covering the horizon began to spit water. I clutched the two envelopes to my chest. I recalled the face of my teenage lover. I decided to confront my memories in the local pub.

I've always been a solitary woman. I tire of people quickly. They bore me. Over the past few years, I got into the habit of having a beer at the Irish pub two blocks from my house. I liked the place because it was normally empty and there were no tourists. Besides which, it had live music. That afternoon I realized that Luis and Vadier had been responsible for my affection for music, for my need of songs. It was only through music that I could lose myself, create meaning, transform my lost causes, dream pipe dreams, and at times, forget my pariah status. I enjoyed listening to the lyrics while doodling on the condensation on the beer glass. I became fond of the Beatles, Jacques Brel, Andrés Calamaro and, to a certain extent, Bob Dylan. Luis—I remembered that afternoon—liked one song in particular very much. Something or other called Johanna, I said to myself. I could never bring myself to listen to it. Many times in shopping malls I would pick up the *Blonde on Blonde* CD. But each time I would suffer an attack of dizziness and usually put it back on the shelf. The musicians at the pub were mostly college students. The majority were temporary acts. The longest lasted three months. I liked watching them strumming guitar strings and imitating the throaty voices of old classic singers. Once, they played "Knockin' on Heaven's Door." That day I recalled Luis. The singers were very young, and in general, they didn't have many Dylan songs in their repertoire. Two or three were standards: "Blowin' in the Wind," "Like a Rolling Stone," and some other random number. I ran my fingers over the envelopes again: inside was something hard, some kind of moveable mass. It was difficult to make out. I avoided the bar. I preferred to sit at a distant table near the washrooms. The fat Canadian guy who'd been playing there the past few months, and who'd sung "Hotel California" a thousand and one times, wasn't on the musician's stool. In his place there was a shaggy-haired kid who looked about sixteen. I had the feeling that he would play something excruciatingly loud and very popular. The waiter greeted me with his usual friendliness. And then, despite my laughable financial state, I ordered a bottle of Blue Label. "What are we celebrating?" he asked, confused. "Nothing," I said, smiling. "It's my anniversary." He went off. He probably told the barman that I was crazy. The kid with the mop of hair tapped the microphone with his fingers a few times, then plucked a few guitar strings. I put the two envelopes down on the table, and with an indefinable sadness, I recalled my teenage

of Johanna that conquer my mind (1:25)." A puppet representing some mediocre film director suspended above a flame. Vadier—a very young-looking Vadier—throwing DVDs into a bonfire. What was the name of that black girl? Nairobi, that's it. "In the empty lot where the ladies play blindman's bluff with the key chain/And the all-night girls whisper of escapades on the D Train/We can hear the night watchman click his flashlight/Asking himself if it's him or them that's insane (2:04)." A game of bowls. A pale, scrawny girl poised in readiness to roll the ball. Claire! Crazy Claire! In the background, Luis, clapping and laughing. In the next photo, Claire and I were jumping up and down in the middle of the patio, celebrating our triumph. A disappointed fat guy was mourning defeat. "Louise, she's all right, she's near/She's delicate and seems like a mirror/But she just makes it perfectly clear/That Johanna's not here (2:22)." I poured myself another shot. The edge of one of the photos got wet from the condensation on the outside of the glass. Nairobi clutching a guitar, a fat girl leaning on her shoulders, and Titina Barca resting her head on my shoulder. "The ghost of 'lectricity howls in the bones of her face... (2:34)." I had the vivid impression that I was driving down a road in a white Fiorino, and if I turned around, I would see Vadier asleep in the back of the car. "Where these visions of Johanna have now taken my place (2:48)." The fat woman, Maigualida—Vadier's friend/lover—trying to cover the lens with her hand. She's laughing. Behind her, two little kids shooting at each other with water pistols. "Now, little boy lost, he takes himself so seriously/He brags of his misery, he likes to live dangerously/And when bringing her name up/He speaks of a farewell kiss to me (3:26)." Green salads:

"But these visions of Johanna, they make it all seem so cruel (5:30)." I downed the shot in a single gulp. The second envelope contained a series of photos taken by Floyd. A yellow sticky note on top of the first one read: *Luis asked me not to let you out of my sight.* Photos from a party. Get-togethers at Nairobi's place. In one, Vadier, Titi, and I are talking on a balcony. "The peddler now speaks to the countess who's pretending to care for him / Sayin', 'Name me someone that's not a parasite and I'll go out and say a prayer for him (5:59).'" Then, pictures of my high school graduation. The principal handing me my diploma. The priest seems to be remonstrating against a disturbance. "But like Louise always says / You just don't get it, do you? / As she, herself, prepares for him / And the Virgin Mary, she still hasn't showed (6:16)." Another photo from the graduation. This time in the college courtyard. Alfonso, with a horrible yellow jacket, is standing next to me, both of us staring at another camera. We're looking elsewhere, giving the impression that I'm whispering something to him. Then, Titina. "The fiddler, he now sets off on the road / He writes, everything's been returned that was owed (6:37)." A series of photos from Titina's illness. She knew it. She knew that Luis had prepared all of this—I could tell from her smile. Titina in her bed at the clinic. A shot of the door: room 1404. In one photo, her bare chest reveals horrible scars; another shows her resting; and in the last shot, she seems to be reluctantly drinking a cloudy juice. "On the back of the fish truck being loaded / While my conscience explodes / The harmonicas play the skeleton keys and the rain (6:54)." The last photo: the airport. There are many people. The blurry image suggests that I'm beating my fist against my chest.

Vadier appears in the background with a puzzled look on his face. "And these visions of Johanna are now all that remain (7:06)." I looked at the photos over and over again. My gaze lingered over every picture, every pixel. The debut artist performed a guitar solo. I don't know why, but out of the blue, I remembered my grandfather Laurent's strange decision to go off and get to know the underworld. You needn't go that far—I said to myself—memory is hell. I wiped my right eye, which had just gone teary. I shoved the photos back inside the envelopes. The song was ending. I poured myself another shot of Blue Label, remembering another expired promise: It's not easy, Titi. No, it's not that easy, I said to the glass. The young kid blew on the harmonica and sang the final verse: "and these visions of Johanna are now all that remain (7:10)."

BONUS TRACK

When, at Vadier's suggestion, I tried to put all these ideas, impressions, good and bad memories, white lies, fabrications, and conscious omissions into some sort of order, it took a lot out of me. My efforts to recall my teenage years landed me in bed for a weekend with a fever of forty degrees. I sorted through the conundrums of my final year of high school, I edited my most humiliating acts of ignorance, and with the help of the internet, I scoured through the contents of the old songbook that my better sense of judgment had banished. El Canto del Loco used to sing "Peter Pan." What crap! How strange time is, I said to myself. I finished putting all this nonsense in some sort of order, and at the top of the first page I wrote: *To Luis Tévez and Cristina Bárcenas.* Then, I pressed Ctrl+S and, following God's example at the end of His creation, I rested.

AFTERWORD

BY ALBERTO BARRERA TYSZKA

In less than two hundred pages, the characters in this book consume twenty-four bottles of Blue Label. That's no mean feat. This is the perfect novel for those with livers of steel. A justification of sorts for a country that for decades has maintained its ranking as the world's number one importer of Scotch whisky. An exercise in patriotic heterogeneity: our national drink is produced four thousand five hundred miles from our territory, mostly based on cereals that we've never seen, under an unknown procedure, and in a language that doesn't belong to us. That's just how we are. The identity of a country is always a paradox. In Venezuela, Johnnie Walker is almost as distinctive as Cacique, our brand of rum.

With skill and creative astuteness, Eduardo Sánchez Rugeles has chosen the metaphor of whisky to carve out a symbolic space within contemporary Venezuelan literature in this difficult beginning to the twenty-first century. But we're not dealing here with a novel about alcoholism, with a series of characters afflicted by addiction. On the contrary.

The whisky in these pages is part of the social norm, the norm of a country that's become accustomed to its narrative as a country on the brink of collapse. In this novel, the consumption of alcohol is not just a personal passion, it's also an anthropological ritual, a collective ceremony, a way of being Venezuelan.

A bottle of Blue Label is a symbol of power, of prestige, of triumph; a political exercise; a way of life; a means of relating to others; and now, thanks to the writing of Sánchez Rugeles, it is also a depiction of failure, of collective boredom as a life project, of a generation whose destiny lies elsewhere. The road trip inland, with twenty-four bottles of whisky in tow, has only one meaning: the need to flee.

The narrative of this novel sets itself a challenging task: teen-girl speak. Sánchez Rugeles has created an uninhibited, adolescent female voice, a character who not only narrates but also provides a rich, raw speech map of Venezuelan youth. However, behind this voice, operating through it, there is also a conscious intent, a creative intelligence that deliberately wants to give language a leading role in the story. The voice encompasses other characters as well, to reflect on what is said and how it's said. The author doesn't want to devote his skills to mere re-creation; he wants to go further, to display the internal architecture of a language, with its sonority and its poverty, with its possibilities and limitations. Choosing orality as a narrative device also demands thinking like another voice.

And indeed it is a different voice—quite distinct. Because the person telling the story of *Blue Label* is also a woman, a girl. And this is probably the greatest challenge and achievement of the novel. Sánchez Rugeles speaks and thinks—he writes—from the female point of view. He varies registers and codes, ranging from the abuse of the word "bitch" to the narrator's relationship with towels; from the interaction with her parents, the relationship with her friends, to the more delicate confessions of love and eroticism. Through her, the novel acquires authenticity and succeeds in making both the female and the male dimension an exploration. Another form of the journey.

But the rhetorical strategy of the female voice, the play of orality, is at the service of an even greater intent: to give sounds, words, a story...to a generation that still has no literary voice of its own. This is the narrative of a group of middle class youths, educated but still biased, full of elements of classism and racism, maintaining a contemptuous distance from the impoverished countryside, desperate to flee a society that they barely know, that they don't understand, but in which they feel profoundly alien. *Blue Label* is a ruthless portrayal of a social class that lived for a long time shunning or shielded from harsh realities. This portrayal allows for the story to be read in another way, even to understand why Chavez came to power. It's the story of the disenchanted. It's the story of those who call Venezuela their home, the country they ignore, before which they feel only disdain or fear.

"In this country, the natural thing is to lose." Young people inherited and adopted this phrase even before putting up a fight. As they move around inside the country, their only real intention is to find a means to get out of the country. Fueled by whisky. The lifeblood of the nation. A whisky that's good for everything. To show power, to establish relationships, to bribe the authorities, to stem religious

TRANSLATOR'S ACKNOWLEDGMENTS

I am grateful to Eduardo Sánchez Rugeles, for his support and encouragement, and to Ruth Greenstein and Turtle Point Press for championing translated literature. I am indebted to Cecilia Egan for her generous editorial support, without which this translation would not have been possible. Sincere thanks also to Montague Kobbé and Celia Wren for their editorial advice. Special thanks to Alicia Filev, for reading drafts and offering suggestions, and to my chess partner Jim for his inspiration and tireless support.

—Paul Filev
Melbourne, January 2018

EDUARDO SÁNCHEZ RUGELES is a fiction writer, screenwriter, and educator. His novels include *Blue Label/Etiqueta Azul*, winner of the Arturo Uslar Pietri Award for Latin American Literature and shortlisted for the Critics Award of Venezuela; *Transylvania, Unplugged*, shortlisted for the Arturo Uslar Pietri Award; *Liubliana*, honorable mention, Sor Juana Inés de la Cruz Bicentennial Literary Award, and winner of the Critics Award of Venezuela; *Jezebel*; and *Julián*. He lives in Madrid.

PAUL FILEV is a Melbourne-based literary translator and editor who translates from Macedonian and Spanish. He was awarded a Literary Translation Fellowship by Dalkey Archive Press in 2015. His translations include Vera Bužarovska's *The Last Summer in the Old Bazaar* and Sasho Dimoski's *Alma Mahler*.